Preying Time

Preying Time

Tracie Loveless-Hill

www.urbanchristianonline.com

Urban Books, LLC
97 N18th Street
Wyandanch, NY 11798

ISBN 13: 978-1-60162-671-4
ISBN 10: 1-60162-671-1

First Trade Paperback Printing July 2014
Printed in the United States of America

10 9 8 7 6 5 4 3 2 1

This is a work of fiction. Any references or similarities to actual events, real people, living or dead, or to real locales are intended to give the novel a sense of reality. Any similarity in other names, characters, places, and incidents is entirely coincidental.

Distributed by Kensington Corp.
Submit Wholesale Orders to:
Kensington Publishing Corp.
C/O Penguin Group (USA) Inc.
Attention: Order Processing
405 Murray Hill Parkway
East Rutherford, NJ 07073-2316
Phone: 1-800-526-0275
Fax: 1-800-227-9604

Preying Time

Tracie Loveless-Hill

Dedication

This novel is dedicated to the memory of my grandmother, Mother Charlie Mae Ambrose, who passed away September 2, 2004. She was the inspiration for Mother Wiley.

Granny, you taught me so many things, too many to list right now. You taught me how to cook and how to sew. You taught me to act and carry myself like a well-mannered and cultured lady. You taught me to love and to give unselfishly with my heart. Words like *compassion* and *empathy* were not only spoken by you, but they were exercised. You taught me to love people for who and what they are, and you showed me how to forgive. You taught me to love my community—and not to just sit back and complain about the problems, but to get up, become active, and do something about them. You told me that obedience is better than sacrifice, and you taught me how to hold on when things get rough and when to let go. You taught me strength and courage and assured me that there is always a positive way to attain what you desire out of life. You gave me an appreciation for the old and a love for antiques.

Granny, most importantly, you taught me about the unmovable, unselfish, and undying love of Jesus Christ. My wish is that my light will shine as brightly as yours, and my hope is to give someone what you have given to me. One of the hardest things that I have ever had to do so far was to let go of your hand that warm early September morning. But, Granny, I will never let go of the things that you have instilled in me. You will be deeply missed and forever loved. And you will live on in my heart and in my work.

Your forever grateful granddaughter, Tracie

Acknowledgments

We are all blessed with special talents and gifts from God. It is up to us to share them with the world, the ones we love, or to just sit on them. I would like to thank the Most High God for giving me the ability to tell a story. It is through Him that all things in my life are possible. To my rock, my love, my husband, Cedric Hill, who has always been so supportive of all my dreams, aspirations, and endeavors. Thank you, and I love you with all my heart. To my children, Taneya and Cedric. You continue to uplift me in those times when I may forget the importance of life's journey. Oh, how I love you with everything in me. And to my sister and my very best friend, Kathy Thomas. You have always had confidence in your big sister and continue to push me and remind me that there is nothing in this world that we cannot accomplish together. Thank you for pushing me to continue to tell my stories.

To my very dear friend and a man of God, Minister Rodger Brown. No matter what it is, I can always call on you, my brother. I'm so grateful to have you as my friend. My dear friends Von Knight and Mildred Holt, thank you for being there for me when I needed you the most. I thank God for that little college campus in Holly Springs, Mississippi, which forged a bond that will never be broken. Cheryl may be gone, but she will live forever in our hearts and memories. Thank you to Randy and Sharon for having four wonderful children. And my gratitude goes to Tricia Spates and Carolyn Mayo for giving me great ideas and memories. I love you, and I thank God for you. And to the lovely ladies of BaHar, how do I say thank you for nurturing my first steps? And lastly to my agent Dr. Maxine Thompson of Black Butterfly Press Literary Agency. May He continue to hold us all in His loving arms.

Tracie Loveless-Hill

What Others Are Saying About
Preying Time

This book has a lot of action, life lessons and enter-tainment. It held my attention to the very last page. The characters were all people that I can relate to because this is such an everyday story. I thoroughly enjoyed reading it.
—Mary Monroe, author of *The Upper Room, God Don't Like Ugly,* and many more great books

This book is very difficult to put down without the com-plete reading. The author does a great job of maintaining your attention, keeping you in suspense, while causing you to do a personal search. A must read for people who desire more strength and a Christian understanding of daily living.
—Dr. Gloria Kirkland Holmes, PhD, University of Northern Iowa, and a pastor's wife

Chapter 1

"Let the church say amen," I said as the pastor of Unity Missionary Baptist Church. "And let's all remember the sick and shut in. And let's say a very special prayer for our dear mother Wiley, who, we all know, would be here tonight if she could. She would be right here, working hard for the Lord."

Taking the purple silk handkerchief from the podium, I wiped the droplets of perspiration that had formed on my forehead. Then I asked, "Are there any more announcements?" as I took a second to look out at the congregation. I scanned the beautiful Unity Missionary Baptist Church, with its magnificent royal blue, gold and it's oak wood color scheme. It was a little piece of heaven right here on earth, I thought. "No more announcements? Good. Then let us all stand for the benediction."

After service, I walked to my office. Loosening my tie, I couldn't help feeling that this has been a long, strenuous day. All I wanted to do was go home, relax in my recliner, and get some rest. My temples were throbbing, so I took several deep breaths as I looked in my desk drawer for some aspirin. I was sitting at my desk, rubbing my temples, when a knock at the door diverted my attention. "Now what?" I said under my breath. "Come in!" I yelled.

"Sorry to bother you, Pastor, but I was wondering if we could talk before you go home this evening."

"Well, Sister Dixon, can't it wait? I'm quite tired. And—"

"I don't think so, Pastor," she said, cutting me off. "You keep putting me off, and we really do need to talk."

This was becoming too much for me. "Okay, Grace. Is tomorrow all right? Sister Harris is waiting for me, and I'm exhausted. How about in the afternoon?" I said, checking my agenda. "I'm having lunch with Reverend Cole and Reverend Leonard. I can come by around one fifteen or one thirty."

"Look, tomorrow will come, and you will not show up. You always do this sort of thing to me," she said between clenched teeth.

"Tomorrow," I insisted, raising my voice, hoping that she would back down.

Leaning over my desk so that her nose was almost touching mine, and piercing me with her big brown eyes, she said angrily, "Tomorrow or else."

A few seconds of silence passed, during which she blew her breath through gritted teeth, and then she turned quickly and walked out of the office, slamming the door behind her.

Grace was very complex. On the one hand, she was one of the sweetest young ladies in my congregation, but if you made her mad, she could be very hard to get along with. I realized this when I began counseling her right after her mother passed. Her outburst only made the pounding in my head worse.

I searched the desk drawer for aspirin again, but I came up empty. Grabbing my jacket from the coatrack, I checked my pocket for my keys, walked out of my office, and locked up. When I stepped out into the sanctuary, there were a few members still hanging around, gossiping. I had noticed before that a few of my members liked to linger after service and talk with one another, a habit that irked me. I spoke briefly to a few members and even hugged a couple of them as I made my way to where my wife was standing.

Teri and I had been married for seven years now, and she was still one of the most beautiful women I had ever laid eyes on. Her skin was the color of buttery pecan and her eyes . . . oh, those hazel eyes.

Her smile was like sunshine, and it would cause her dimples to appear like a rainbow after a storm. She kept her hair long enough to delicately frame her oval face. And hers was the face of an angel. She never had to work very hard to maintain her gorgeous five-foot-ten figure. Since the first time I laid eyes on her, she had always stood tall and regal. Teri Harris was the perfect woman for any good man, for me.

We met in college. I remembered that she had always had her head stuck in a book. I would do everything I could think of to get her to notice me, but she didn't, until one day after a football practice. Coach Stovall had made us practice for two extra hours because we had lost a very important game the weekend before and he was pretty upset about it.

With only a few minutes to go before the serving lines closed in the cafeteria, we had to drag our sore, tired bodies to dinner while we were still in those dirty practice uniforms. No one was trying to be a gentleman; in fact, we were all still upset with Coach. We were so hungry that we didn't realize we had pushed our way through the short line. That was until I heard someone behind me exhale loudly and say, "You are just rude!"

Slightly embarrassed, I turned to say that I was sorry, and that was when I saw that it was Teri Andrews. Now I was really embarrassed and ashamed at the same time.

"Sorry. You can go on ahead of me," I told her.

"No thanks. That's all right," she shot back. "You guys practically knocked me over, trying to get to this food," she scolded.

"No, please," I insisted.

"Well, it is almost closing time, and I'm hungry. But just because you guys are on the football team, that doesn't give you the right to go around being so rude!"

I let her finish. "Now that you've bitten my head off, is there any chance I can make this up to you?"

Her face said it all. "What?" Her hazel eyes gave me the once-over. "What did you just ask me?"

Trying to keep my nerve, I said, "May I please have a chance to make it up to you?" Before she could answer, I told her that I wanted to sit with her during dinner and talk. She was shocked by my candidness, and I have to admit that I was also, but I wasn't going to let the chance to get to know her go by. "I see that you're all alone, and I promise to be a good guy."

This made her smile.

Good, I thought, feeling relieved.

We got our food and found a seat. We talked, and I learned that she was from Chicago, the daughter of a Baptist minister. She was majoring in both sociology and criminology, and she revealed that she one day hoped to work for the federal government. *Great,* I thought as I listened to her talk.

I told her that I was from Memphis and that I was an associate minister at my church. This took her by surprise. I also told her that I had aspirations of becoming a pastor of my own congregation one day.

After dinner I walked her back to her dorm and told her that I would like to see her again. That is, if she could take her head out of her books long enough.

She laughed her bubbly laugh, which I had since grown so fond of. As I gazed into her hazel eyes, she whispered, "Sure."

I was at a loss for words.

"We can eat together tomorrow and talk some more. You are pretty funny, you know," she said as she turned to walk into the front entrance of her dorm.

Quickly regaining my senses, I blurted, "That'll work," before she was inside. "Thank you, Lord," I found myself saying out loud, not caring who might overhear me, as I ran to my dorm to shower and study. I couldn't study or sleep much that night, as I was thinking about those alluring hazel eyes.

And even as I walked up to her today, Teri Harris was still breathtaking to me.

"Sweetheart, I'll walk you over to the parsonage, and then I'll need to leave for a few minutes. I forgot that I have some business to attend to tonight," I told her.

"Oh? Is there anything I can do for you? Would you like for me to go along with you?" she asked, sounding concerned.

"No, sweetheart, there's nothing for you to worry yourself about. Anyway, it should take only a few minutes."

"Are you sure, Randall?" I could see the concern intensifying in her eyes.

I smiled at her. I found her concern touching. I assured her everything was fine and walked her home. Walking back to the parsonage, I looked at her out of the corner of my eye to see if she had bought my story. If she hadn't, it didn't show. She was talking about something that I didn't care to pay attention to. I had only one thing on my mind after the confrontation with Grace.

Chapter 2

I loved my wife with all that I had in me, but I was a man of means . . . and sometimes I needed a little something extra. I have always felt that what you didn't know wouldn't hurt you. And I had always tried my best to shield my wife from my extracurricular activities.

I was called to preach the word at an early age. As a child, I always felt that I had to carry myself in a different manner from the other boys in the neighborhood. No, I never had much time for a girlfriend. It wasn't like the girls were not after me. I was just more into my studies at the time. I was called Mother's golden boy because all the elders of the church thought that I was special. And the parents were always trying to fix their daughters up with me by going through my mother. But she would always politely tell them that I had more important things to do. I felt that I was missing out on a lot of the fun that the other boys were having, but I couldn't disappoint the people of the church. And most certainly not Mama.

After all, I was the Reverend Randall Creighton Harris, pastor of the prestigious Unity Missionary Baptist Church. Yes, I was a man of God, but first and foremost, I was a man—a man who sometimes spread himself just a little too thin. And now I felt it was time for some catch-up—as long as I did not include God in my mess. First of all, I was the secretary for the Ministers Alliance. Second, I was a mentor and counselor for the juvenile delinquency program. Third, I was a member and a past adviser of our local chapter of Omega Psi Phi Fraternity. Lastly, I met at least once a week at the Boys and Girls Club to counsel them on their mentoring program.

I felt that I needed a little something extra tonight, and that something extra was Raychell. Raychell was a young lady who was trying to get through school. She was working on a degree in social work. I sometimes gave her gifts of money to help her out. I called them gifts because I would never think about paying a woman for sex.

When I arrived at her apartment, she was wearing one of those sexy nightgowns that she liked to tease me with. Oh yes, I could see that she had really missed her man. To me, she was really looking good!

Raychell was about five feet four, slim, and the color of dark chocolate. She had the most sensuous mouth I had ever seen on a woman. Her lips were like soft pillows of satin and were a clear sign of her West Indian heritage. Her teeth indicated that she truly believed in oral hygiene, and she had a wickedly sexy smile. Her breasts weren't as large as I would've liked them to be, but they were like perky little melons, the ones that could fit perfectly in my mouth.

I could feel my mouth begin to water as my eyes followed her body downward to her slim yet curvaceous hips, her perfectly rounded butt, and her well-proportioned, slightly bowed legs.

As I walked through her front door, I could see that she had everything set out and waiting for me. The incense was burning, and the weed was on the table.

"How long can you stay tonight?" she asked sadly.

"Not too long," was my answer. "I have a long day ahead of me tomorrow. You know I had to stop over and check on my baby," I continued.

"Well, come on over here and relax for a while. I have everything out and waiting just for you." She walked over to the couch, sat, and patted the pillow next to her. "You do realize that our times together are growing shorter and shorter, don't you?" She readjusted her body on the beige leather couch.

"Yes, but you also know I'm a very busy man with a lot of obligations."

"Do you want to spend more time with me?" She pouted, turning me on even more with her delicious lips.

"You know I do, Ray." I loved to call her that name for short.

"Then give up some of your obligations."

I felt myself getting irritated. "We seem to go through this every time and . . ."

"I know, sweetheart," she said, pulling me toward her on the couch. "Just let me take care of you right here, right now, tonight," she whispered as she placed burning kisses on my face and neck. When I relaxed all my senses, she sat up. I watched carefully as she placed a cigar in her mouth and flicked the lighter. "Here. Take this," she said, handing me the lit blunt. "Let me massage your shoulders for you."

I took slow, deep pulls from the weed-packed cigar, held the smoke in my lungs for a few seconds, and then exhaled.

"Ahh, yeah, baby . . . I don't know what I would do without you."

"Same here," she said. "You can't blame me for wanting to spend more time with you." She flicked my ear with her tongue.

"I would love to take you out places. I would love to be able to wake up beside you in the mornings and do all those things that lovers do, but you know the position I'm in."

"You mean do all the things that you and your wife do?"

"Ray!" She knew that Teri was definitely not a subject to be discussed. She backed off when she felt my body stiffen.

"Oh, baby, I need you." She resumed kissing my neck. "Come on. I can't wait to get to the room."

After placing the blunt in the ashtray on her ivory, glass, and marble table, I began to loosen my belt as she pushed the table away with her foot. She helped unbutton my shirt.

"Hurry," she whispered in my ear as she guided me to her fluffy beige area rug. "I've missed you so much." She began to place hot kisses on my chest. Her soft lips worked their way downward, and I almost lost it when she stuck her hot tongue in and out of my navel.

"Oh, my goodness," I tried to say.

"Shhh." She put her index finger over my lips, her French-tipped nail lightly rubbing across my upper lip, sending shivers through me at full speed. She understood that I was almost at my peak when she sat up and gazed into my eyes while removing her nightgown. Never taking her eyes away from mine, she slowly glided her body on top of mine. I closed my eyes as her sensual body welcomed mine.

"Don't say a word," she whispered as she began to move slowly to the music that was playing on her stereo. The music began to speed up, and so did she. As she worked her body into a frenzy, I could no longer hold back. We were both soon entangled in a sweat-soaked mess in the middle of her living room floor.

"Oh, my goodness," I said, out of breath. I struggled to push myself up so that I could sit and lean against her couch. "Do you have anything to drink? I'm a little dehydrated or something. I swear, girl, you wear me out every time."

"I'd like to wear you out more often," she commented as she rose and walked into the kitchen.

I chuckled and gathered my clothes, which I'd discarded all over her floor.

"Would you like to take a shower or a bath tonight?" she asked as she handed me a cold glass of water.

After taking the glass in my hand and quickly gulping down its contents, I finally answered, "A quick shower please." Handing the glass back, I said, "Ray, I just really needed to see you tonight."

"So would you like for me to take a shower with you?" she asked.

"Come over here," I said. Rubbing my thumb across her lips, I told her, "Now, you know that I would never get out of here if you did that." Looking into her eyes, I could see her motive. "Are you trying to get me to stay on purpose?"

"Forget it," she snapped, hurt in her eyes now, as she walked toward the bathroom. "I'll run you a stupid shower."

"Ray, baby," I said, but she was no longer listening.

When I had finished my shower, put my clothes on, and returned to the dining room, she was sitting at the table, pretending to study.

"I'll see you later this week, okay?" I said.

She ignored me.

"Ray, did you hear what I said?"

"Sure," she answered, never looking up from her books.

"Look, baby—"

"No, you don't have to explain anything to me," she said, cutting me off. "I knew exactly what I was getting myself into when I started this with you. I'm fine," she said. "You just go on home to your wife."

Irritated, I turned to leave. I was walking toward the door when she said, "Oh, by the way, this week won't work for me. I'm going to be pretty busy myself." She never looked up from her books.

I walked out the door and slammed it behind me without saying another word.

On the ride home I was happy to see that the traffic was light. The air was clean and refreshing to my lungs. The stars in the sky were beautiful. As crazy as it sounded, it reminded me of Teri's eyes. But what was I going to say to my wife if she was still awake? She hardly questioned me about what I did. But every now and then she would surprise me. As I drove into the garage, I was glad to see that most of the lights in the house were out. I walked into the kitchen, threw my keys on the island, and then tiptoed into the bedroom.

Good. Teri was sound asleep. I didn't feel much like trying to explain to her where I had been.

"Honey, is that you?" she asked, half asleep.

"Go on back to sleep, my dear. I didn't mean to wake you," I said, slipping under the covers.

"Did you take care of your business, sweetheart?"

"What? Oh, yeah, I did," I mumbled.

Before I could utter another sentence, she was softly snoring again. This was a great relief. I didn't feel like coming up with a lie tonight. I was exhausted. And I hated lying to her, but what was a man to do?

Chapter 3

"Thank you, Reverend Cole, and thank you, Reverend Leonard," I said, "for meeting me for lunch today."

Both men really seemed to be enjoying the day's special of fried chicken, turnip greens, black-eyed peas, corn on the cob, and hot buttered corn bread. We were washing it down with some of Sister Annie Mae's honey-sweetened iced tea.

Reverend Cole was the pastor of Revelation Missionary Baptist Church and was somewhat new to our community. He was short and very plump, with a bald head. When he walked, he made me think of a duck waddling. Reverend Leonard was the pastor of Bethel A.M.E. He was the opposite of Reverend Cole in terms of his appearance, as he was tall and slim. Both had small congregations, but the Ministers Alliance could use both of them, for they both were very moving orators.

"I think the Ministers Alliance will greatly appreciate your participation this year, brothers. We are kicking off a fund-raiser to add additional rooms to the center. Next week our treasurer, Reverend Evans of Mt. Sinai Baptist, should be able to join us, and maybe we can get this ball rolling," I commented.

"Well, Reverend Harris, this is really a great program for the community. I really like the fact that the Alliance has attorneys lined up for the underprivileged. The kids out here today need someone to speak up for them, because they surely do not know how to represent them-

selves well at all when it comes to the justice system."
Reverend Cole wiped his mouth with a napkin. "I, for one,
feel blessed to take part in it, very blessed."

I wanted to question him about where he had gotten
such close-minded opinions, but as I watched him eat his
meal, I opted against it.

"Amen!" added Reverend Leonard.

"Well, gentlemen, with news like this, I think that I will
just take care of the tab for both of you," I said, pushing
my chair back from the table.

"Oh, well, then, in that case I will meet you for lunch
every Monday." Reverend Leonard laughed.

We all laughed a hearty laugh as Annie Mae Griffin
came over to our table.

"So how was everything, Pastor? Gentlemen?" she
asked as she waved to someone to come and clear our
table. "I do hope that everything was satisfactory."

Annie Mae's Soul Food Restaurant was small, and it
did not have the most attractive atmosphere, with its dull,
cream-colored walls and its brown-and-white checkered
curtains and matching table coverings. The tables were
small and had been placed too close together, but the
place was always packed with good people and good
conversation. The food was even better.

"Oh, yes, just wonderful, Sister Griffin," I replied.
"Everything was delicious, as always."

"You don't ever have to worry about losing any business," added Reverend Cole, with grease still around his
upper lip. "Sister, you are surely blessed."

"Why, thank you, Reverend. I just hope that it will keep
you coming back." Annie Mae smiled widely.

"Sister Griffin, if your cooks continue to cook like this,
we will always come back," Reverend Cole assured her.

"Wonderful!" She continued to smile. "I'll just take the
check and meet you men at the register. I just wanted to
stop over and say howdy to my pastor here."

I quickly slipped her two twenty-dollar bills and told her to keep the change.

"Bless you, Pastor," she squealed as she slid her way to the front, where the register was located.

Standing, I informed the reverends that I had another meeting to attend. We all shook hands, agreed to meet at the same time and place next week, then said our good-byes and went our separate ways.

En route to Grace's house, I picked up my cell phone to call Teri but then decided against it. She would probably begin asking questions that I was not in the mood to answer. Traffic was fair for a Monday afternoon, and I got to Grace's house before I realized it.

Finding a parking spot in front of the small brick home was easy in this working poor neighborhood. I suspected that most folks were hard at work. I noticed that a few children who were not yet old enough for school were out playing in their front yards, while some of the mothers were sitting on their porches. This neighborhood reminded me a lot of the one where I grew up. A few yards were kept to the best of their owners' abilities, but junk cars helped to litter some of the other yards. Freshly washed clothes hung on rope lines, and everybody knew everybody else's business. I could definitely say that I had come a mighty long way from that life. Although those days were long gone, I did have some fond memories of my mother.

Just as my mind began to wander, I looked over toward Grace's house, and it brought me back to the real reason I was here.

"Lord, please give me the strength," I said, looking up to the skies.

As I walked up to the front door, a police car drove past, the officer eyeing me from head to toe. I wonder what in the world could be so important that Grace had to be so insistent. We had both agreed to break off the little fling that we had had a few months back. As I went to ring the doorbell, the front door swung open, and I could tell by the look on her face that this was not going to be a comfortable meeting.

"Good afternoon, Sister Dixon—" I said before she cut me off.

"Cut the crap. My father is not at home. I'm here alone." She paused and looked me up and down. "He's still working a lot of overtime, so I don't expect him until much later."

"So are we going to just stand here, or are you going to let me in?" I asked, confused.

Once again, she looked me up and down, with a look on her face like she had just tasted something unpleasant. She backed up just enough so that I could walk past her into the small living room.

"Your father has been working quite a bit of overtime lately, hasn't he?" I asked just to keep the conversation going on a smooth level.

"Yeah, that's all he seems to do since Mama died," she answered, sitting in a lounge chair across from me. I was sitting on the couch in front of the window. "It's like he doesn't like being in this house anymore," she said.

"So, Grace, what's so important?" I asked. Not really sure if I wanted to hear what she had to say, I braced myself. Things were quiet for a few seconds, so I cleared my throat to break the silence.

"Reverend Harris," she began, almost in tears, "we have a serious problem."

Sitting back on the couch, I continued to brace myself for what was about to come. I waited about thirty seconds, but she didn't continue. "Well, are you going to tell me, or am I going to have to guess?" I finally asked, irritated. I could see that her eyes were red and tears had begun to run down her face. "What is it, Grace?" I asked. I was really becoming upset myself at this point. "Whatever it is, I'm sure that it can't be that bad. Or is it?"

Looking up and into my eyes, she answered in a whisper, "I'm pregnant."

"Excuse me?" I said and stood up at the same time. "Pregnant? By whom?" My voice rose uncontrollably.

She gave me a look as if she wanted to kill me. "By *whom?* You want to know by whom? Who in the world do you think?"

"I d-don't know," I stuttered.

"It's yours, that's who!"

"But, Grace, I haven't been with you in over two months, and you told me that you were always protected!"

"I've been trying to talk to you for almost a month now, but you kept putting me off, remember?"

"How do you know it's mine?"

"Because you're the only person I was sleeping with. That's how I know!"

"I don't believe you," I shouted. "I mean, you were not a virgin when I got with you. How am I supposed to believe you about this? You've got to be lying. Come on, Grace, why me?"

"Why you? Why *you?*" she shouted through her tears. "What about me? Just think about how my father is going to feel about this. I wanted to go to college or join the air force. It's not all about you, you know."

"I don't believe this. Why are you trying to pin this on me? Why do you want to hurt me when all I ever did was try to help you?"

She was uncontrollable at this point. "Help me? You were trying to help me?" She blew out a heavy sigh. "I'm not doing anything to hurt you. The way I see it, we are both responsible for this situation, and I just felt you had a right to know."

"What about an abortion?" I asked, pacing the floor of the small room. "Have you given that any thought?"

Her crying stopped. "I'm not killing my baby. I've been walking around in a daze since the day I found out. My dad is going to be so upset. And he is going to want to know who is responsible. I may not have any plans right now, but I do know that I'm not going to kill my baby," she warned me.

"Well, we are going to have to do something and . . ." I paused. "Do you know what would happen if the church found out? If my wife found out?" I decided at that moment that I had had enough of this conversation.

As I headed for the door, I could hear that she had started sobbing again. "I just thought that I should tell you before I told my father. I haven't even figured out what I'm going to say to him yet." She boo-hooed.

I was paralyzed, and I felt as if I was drowning from this news that I had been given. In a pleading voice I asked once more, "Grace, are you sure that it's mine?"

"I think you should leave now," was her answer. She composed herself as best she could and looked down at the floor. She seemed to have sunk deep into thought.

Walking to my car, I knew that I had the expression of a deer caught in headlights. I couldn't even get the key to go into the ignition right away. "This just cannot be happening to me, not now," I said aloud as I started the engine of my silver Cadillac and drove down the street. "Oh, my goodness, Brother Dixon is going to lose his mind when she tells him. No, he is going to rip my head off. What have I gotten myself into?"

Brother Dixon was a good, hardworking man who had been devoted to his wife of twenty years. She had died of uterine cancer eight short months ago. He was a very quiet man, a man who was difficult to read. All that I could tell about him was that his family and the church were his world. Now that his wife was gone, he worked overtime to keep himself busy. How was he going to react to this? *Oh, what am I going to do now?* I thought. *This could destroy everything that I've worked so hard to build up. I can't lose Unity Missionary Baptist Church, and I can't lose my wife.*

I thought back to the first day my wife and I came there. I thought that the church was one of the most magnificent buildings I had ever seen. The structure would lead one to believe it was built for a king. I could see right away that it held over a thousand members, and I had plans to fill every pew. The colors of the interior took my breath away. That royal blue, and gold looked so beautiful together. I knew right off that some of the members would give me a run for my money. After all, I was a young man who was stepping into a much older man's shoes. But most of the congregation welcomed Sister Harris and me with open and loving arms. Yes, it was an uphill battle in the beginning, but together we had become a strong church family. We had also made Unity one of the most prestigious churches in the city. I just couldn't be on the verge of losing it all.

After driving around for a while, I decided to return to my office. I had too much on my mind to get any work done, so I decided to call my closest friend, Deacon Samuel Wise.

Brother Sam, as I called him, didn't know everything about me, but he knew enough to hurt me if he wanted to. I had learned a long time ago that you should never let one person find out too much about you. No man could keep a secret completely. One wise old preacher had once told me that if you told your business, then you were also telling someone else's. In this business, you had to remain careful. But I felt that I needed to talk to someone right then and now.

In the past, anytime that I ran into any problems and needed him, all I had to do was call. He was always right there for me. But this was not what I would consider a small problem. When my car was seen at the motel by the mall, Brother Sam took the blame for that. When the police came around snooping because of my ties to a local drug dealer, Brother Sam helped me to straighten that out also. And years ago, when Teri went to visit her family and she could not reach me, he told her that the church and the parsonage were having phone trouble all that week. He had certainly gotten my butt out of a sling many times over, but this time was different.

Dialing his number, I lost my nerve and was just about to hang up when a soft voice came over the receiver.

"Good afternoon, Sister Wise. How are you this blessed day?" I asked.

"Oh, Pastor Harris, I'm doing just fine today. I'm trying to catch a cold, though. I've been trying to fight it for the past week, but I tell you that the devil is a liar."

Yeah, yeah, yeah, I thought. "Well, we are going to have to pray that ole devil off of you, sister," I said, half concerned.

"Thank you, Pastor," she returned. "Now, how is Sister Harris?" she went on. This was when I remembered how Sister Wise loved to talk.

"We are both blessed and doing just fine."

"Praise the Lord!"

"Yes. Sister, I was calling to see if the deacon was around."

"No, Pastor. He had an appointment with someone about some business at the shop."

"I hope everything is going okay with the shop," I said with some concern. Now, I should have known that he would be at the shop this time of day, I thought.

"Yes, sir, everything is fine. He went into the auto shop early this morning because of the meeting, but I expect him home at the regular time, between five and six. Should I tell him to call you when he gets in?"

"No, Sister, don't worry about it. I can reach him later on at the shop. You just try to enjoy the rest of your day," I told her before hanging up the phone.

I knew that she could keep me on the phone all day if I had let her. Maybe it was good that the deacon wasn't at home. This was a problem that I was going to have to work out for myself.

Chapter 4

When I got home that evening, Teri was stretched out on the couch in the blue room, reading a book. Peering at me over her novel, she could sense that I had had a pretty rough day.

"Hey, sweetie," she said, beaming. "I didn't know that you were coming home this early. Are you hungry? I can fix something for you," she continued as she stretched and laid her book on the coffee table.

Just as she began to rise, I told her to sit and assured her that I was not hungry.

"Oh, aren't you feeling well?" She walked over to were I was anyway.

"I'm just a little tired, I guess," I answered as I looked through the mail on the kitchen island.

"Can I get you a glass of juice? You should have something."

"No, Teri," I answered, getting a bit irritated. "I'm just fine. Now, go on doing whatever it was that you were doing."

She stared at me as if she could see right through me; I immediately regretted raising my voice.

"I'm sorry, honey. I'm just really tired, is all. I think I'm going to go and lie down for a while. I'm so sorry," I said, softly kissing her on the cheek.

"All right, darling. You go and lie down. I've got some calls to make, anyway. I hadn't realized how much time had gone by. I'll let you get some rest now. Just call me if you need anything, love." She kissed me on my lips and hugged me around my waist. She stared into my eyes with those hazel jewels that made me weak in the knees. "I love you," she cooed, kissing me once more on the lips. Then she turned and walked around the kitchen island.

I was almost frozen in place, watching her glide about the kitchen the way that she did. *I can't lose this*, I thought.

Finally, I moved in the direction of the master bedroom. I took off my tie, shirt, belt, shoes, socks, and pants, letting everything fall on the floor. I slipped into a pair of sweatpants and lay across the enormous bed. I must have been drained by the day's events, because before I knew it, I was out like a light. My bladder awakened me sometime in the middle of the night to inform me that I needed to take a much-needed trip to the bathroom. I saw that Teri had picked up the clothes I had let fall, and had dutifully put them away. I looked at her as she softly snored next to me and wondered, what in the world would I do without her? What would I do without her love and support?

Chapter 5

After waking up last night, I couldn't go back to sleep. I just lay there listening to Teri sleep, trying to figure a way out of this mess I'd gotten myself into. *Lord, how am I going to get out of this one? What have I done?* I thought. Sometimes I allowed things to go a little too far.

While driving to the office, I decided that maybe I could look up Monica and she could tell me what was going on with Cornell Hollis. That boy had always been trouble, and as far as I was concerned, he would always be trouble. Yes, maybe he was the answer that I was looking for.

I had known Monica for about five years now. She worked for the juvenile probation office. She had graduated from Spelman in Atlanta. In fact, all her sisters and her mother had graduated from Spelman. Monica was both smart and pretty, and she loved nothing more than for people to tell her this.

She had been married for twelve years, I believed. But she was always complaining about being underappreciated by her husband. Her clueless husband, Michael, was a very driven man—driven to keep her fingers full of diamonds and her neck warm with furs, driven to keep her in a beautiful three-level home while driving a Lexus, driven to keep her in a lifestyle that most people could only dream about. He was working himself to death trying to keep her happy. He traveled and was away from home a lot, which left her with a lot of free time on her hands.

Since he wasn't there on a daily basis to tell her that she was beautiful and special, I did it for him. Just a few strokes of the ego, and I was in her bed. I'd just give her a call and maybe find out what Cornell was up to.

Bringing up her number on my cell, I pushed send. After a couple of rings, she answered. "Monica Levy's office."

"Hello, beautiful. How is this morning treating you?" I was trying my best to sound interested.

"Things are a little slow around here this morning, but I'm booked solid this afternoon with meetings. How is your morning?" she asked.

"I was just thinking about you. I can't seem to get you out of my mind lately. When can I see you?"

"Excuse me," she returned in her professional tone, her little cue to let me know that someone was around.

"Oh, I see you have someone in your office."

"That's right."

"Okay, then I'll let you go for now, but I do want to see you tonight. Please," I whined like a small child.

"Sure. Is seven all right?"

"Oh, you can't make it any sooner than that, gorgeous?"

"Okay, seven is fine. You know the place. I'll see you there," she said, trying to remain in her professional mode.

"I'll be there . . . and I can't wait to see you, sexy," I cooed into the receiver.

"Sure, and thanks for reminding me. I'll see you tonight."

Then the line went dead. As I put my phone back in my pocket, I thought back to the day that I met Monica at the courthouse. She was there with a client, and I was there for a meeting with the county attorney. When the elevator door opened and she stepped in, I thought she had the most gorgeous head of hair. Her face was about 50 percent makeup, but I could still see that underneath it all she was still a fairly attractive woman.

Monica stood about five feet seven, and she had large breasts, which she loved to display. Her waist and her hips were about the same measurement, so I tried to focus just on her hair and breasts. She had a high forehead and liked to brush her hair back the way that the singer Sade wore hers. I had to admit that I did indeed love to run my fingers through her mane. Those long, shiny, silky black tresses . . . I was like a kid playing with one of his favorite toys. . . .

I had let my mind wander. I had better call Teri to let her know that I'd be late coming home this evening.

My little hideaway with Monica was a small motel about fifteen miles out of town. She seemed to snub it at first, but she came to like it for its cute, cozy qualities. Our usual room had a queen-size bed, a big-screen television, and a Jacuzzi. She liked to sit in the Jacuzzi in her swimsuit. I guess in her mind she had the bomb body. Who was I to object? I would just compliment her and play in her hair.

Driving into the motel parking lot just before seven, I noticed that Monica's Lexus was parked in its usual spot. I had better make this good, I thought as I swung into my spot next to hers.

When I knocked on the door, she peeked through the security peephole as if she didn't know that it would be me.

"It's me," I told her.

As she opened the door, I could see that she had brought a swimsuit, and it was hugging her body like a glove.

"You look like a million bucks," I lied as she tried to prance around the room so that I could get a better look.

"Thanks. I picked this little number up after work this evening just for you. I thought you would appreciate it," she professed boldly.

"Oh, you were wrong, baby. I love it," I lied. "Is Michael out of town again?"

"Of course," she answered with a wave of her hand, wanting me to change the subject. "I didn't come here to talk about Michael. I came here to be romanced by a very handsome man," she said between kisses on my bottom lip.

"Well, my lady, your wish is my command." I grinned. "You know I just love to make you happy."

She sat down on the edge of the bed, grabbed her glass, and began to sip some cognac. "Would you like a drink?"

"Sure, but very little. I don't want to go home smelling like cognac tonight," I replied as I sat on the bed.

"Oh, don't worry. I'm going to make sure you don't get drunk tonight, lover, because I want to enjoy every minute that I have with you. And I want you sober."

She poured me a drink, then sat next to me and handed me the glass. I took a large gulp and closed my eyes, trying to shut out everything that was going on outside the room. Placing what was left of my drink on the nightstand, I forced myself to look into her eyes.

"You know that I can't stand to be away from you, Monica. Your beauty captivates me."

She lay back on the bed and let her hair fall over the bedspread. The cognac gave me the nerve to dish out the compliments that her ego craved so desperately.

"How long are you going to be able to stay with me tonight, Randall?" Thanks to her superior, overinflated image of herself, she could not even allow herself to call me by my title. I usually just let it roll off, but it was starting to get on my nerves. If we were going to deal much longer, she was going to have to show me some respect.

"For a while," I answered.

"But not long," she said as she got up from the bed. She walked into the bathroom.

"Monica, dear, you know my situation. Please let us not ruin the precious time that we do have together," I pleaded.

"I'm not," she answered through the door. "It's just that I plan on staying overnight myself and leaving here for work in the morning."

"I see. . . . Well, the sooner you're in my arms, the better."

When she opened the door, I saw that she had removed her swimsuit. "I was just making sure my protection was right," she told me before climbing into the bed.

"You take care of everything, love. I never have to worry about you, do I?"

"We'll both have a lot to lose if something should happen," she whispered as she kissed my neck and unbuttoned my shirt. "Just let me give you what I've been wanting to give you for a long time." She stuck her tongue in my ear.

I tingled from her warm breath. The cognac helped also. After what seemed like hours of lovemaking, I glanced over at the clock. It revealed that it had been more like six minutes. I was exhausted. She grabbed her robe and got up to fix herself another drink.

"I can fix you another one," she said, turning to face me.

"No, thanks," I responded, still out of breath. "I told you I cannot drink too much tonight. I have to drive back into the city."

"Well, what about some more lovemaking? You know I don't get to see you all that much," she coaxed as she sipped on her drink.

"You never cease to amaze me, Monica." I laughed. "Here I am, still out of breath. Once again you have drained me. But if you don't mind, I would like for you to lay your sexy body next to me for a while."

"Sure," she said with a smile as she cuddled up next to me.

After five or so minutes of silence, I got ready to take a quick shower. I felt that this was a good time to put my plan into action.

"Hey, Monica, do you remember that one kid, Cornell, whose grandmother goes to my church? You worked as his caseworker a while back, when he was a juvenile," I said.

"Who? Cornell Hollis?"

"Yeah, that's him—Sister Hollis's grandson. Has he been keeping out of trouble?"

"I guess he has been trying to, as far as his grandmother will admit to me. Why? Has his grandmother complained about something?" she asked, never letting up on her drinking.

"No, she hasn't. It's just that she hasn't been in church for a few weeks. I know that when he was released from lockup, he and his mother had to move back in with her. I wonder if I should have a talk with him about coming to church."

Choosing to ignore what I was saying, she asked if she could join me in the shower. That was the one thing I could always count on from Monica. Monica's only concern was Monica and Monica only.

"Now you really want to get me into trouble, don't you, gorgeous?" *Okay, enough of this mess,* I thought.

"Oh, just go on. You're such a spoilsport," she retorted, then grabbed the television remote and began scanning the channels. "Go on and take your shower and leave." She acted like she was pouting now.

"Come on, don't be like that, baby. You know how I feel about you."

"And you know how I feel about you, Randall, but you aren't any fun anymore. I want things to be like they used to be between us." She continued to pout like the spoiled brat that she was.

"I'm sorry, beautiful. It's just that I have been under a lot of pressure lately. You know with church matters alone, I have been so busy. Please forgive me. *Please?*" I whined.

"Oh, go on, you big baby." She finally smiled.

I showered, kissed her good night, and I was out.

Chapter 6

When I woke up the next morning, Teri had already bathed and left the house. A note on the note board informed me that her friends from her book club were having their monthly meeting at our house this evening. Shoot, I had forgotten that this was her month to host the book club. I couldn't keep up with all her ridiculousness. How in the world could she stay so busy doing nothing? I would never figure it out. I tossed her note into the wastebasket and head into the kitchen.

She had left my breakfast in the microwave. I was not in the mood for waffles, so I just ate the sausage patties and poured myself a glass of cranberry juice. Going through the morning paper, it hit me, and I couldn't concentrate on the day's news right now, so I lay the paper aside. I needed to get in touch with Cornell Hollis, and I need to convince Grace to keep her mouth shut until I could come up with a plan to get myself out of this mess we had made.

Grabbing the phone from the kitchen island, I quickly dialed Grace's number. She answered in a tired voice.

"Good morning, Sister Dixon—"

"Yeah?" she said, cutting me off quickly.

"Well, how are you feeling this morning?" I asked, trying to sound concerned. "Have you spoken with your father yet?"

After a long and heavy sigh, she answered, "No. He's been so tired lately that I've just been waiting for the right time."

"Well, can I ask you to do me a favor?"

The line was dead silent.

"Can I ask you not to tell him too soon? I think we can come up with another way to handle this," I told her.

"I told you that I was not getting an abortion." Her voice rose as she spoke, and I had to move the receiver away from my ear. "I thought I had made myself clear about that."

"Yes, you did, and I am not talking about an abortion, either."

"Then what are you talking about? I know you aren't going to leave your wife," she said sarcastically.

Her words stung just a bit. I hated it when they had to bring my wife into it. But I forced a laugh. "I just want to make sure we can come up with a solution for this."

"Well, I'm going to have to tell him real soon, because I'm already two months going on three and everybody will know pretty soon," she said.

"I know this, Grace, but please, I'm just asking you for a little more time, all right? Please don't say anything until I have a chance to speak with you again. Okay?"

After a long pause she agreed to do as I'd asked. After thanking her and giving her the false sense that I cared, I hung up the phone. Since I was not in my office, where all the church members' information was stored, I had to search around the house for a phone book. Once I found it, I hurriedly looked up the number for Ethel Hollis.

Sister Hollis was a nice lady, but she was just a little too nosy for my taste. She was always in someone's business. But when her crackhead daughter got picked up for soliciting or those grandsons of hers got into any trouble, her mouth was like Fort Knox.

"Good. The number is listed," I caught myself saying. I dialed the number, thinking about what I was going to say to Cornell.

"Good morning, Sister Hollis," I said when I recognized the voice of the person who had answered the phone. "This is your pastor calling to check up on you. I've noticed that you haven't been to church lately, and I was worried about one of my favorite members," I lied.

"Oh, Pastor Harris," she replied with surprise in her tone. "How are you and your beautiful wife?"

"Now, sister, we are just fine, but I'm calling to see how you're getting along."

"Well, my asthma has been giving me the fits, you know? And I am an old lady and all. It just seems a little harder to shake these things off nowadays."

"Well, we're going to have to see to it that you get better, Sister Hollis, because I really do miss you at church."

"Oh, Pastor." She giggled like a schoolgirl. "You sure do know how to make an old lady feel good. Bless your heart."

"And you, Sister, are missed. Is there anything I can do for you?" I asked.

"No, sir. My daughter, Corine, and her two boys have been staying with me for a while, and between the three of them, I am doing just fine," she told me.

I bet you are, was my thought. I know her daughter and her grandsons, and they were probably robbing her blind. "Wonderful then. I'm just glad you're not over in that big house all alone."

"No, sir, there is always something going on around here." She laughed.

"How is that grandson of yours doing? The one that was in Madison State School?" I asked.

"Cornell is supposed to be in school today. He's been trying his best to stay out of trouble. If only I could get him to stay away from them bad boys out there in those streets, he will be all right." I could hear disgust in her voice. "I just can't seem to talk to him anymore, you know? Maybe you can get through to him somehow, Pastor."

"I would love to give it a try, Sister Hollis. Would you please tell him that I want to talk with him? Let me give you my cell number, just in case I'm away from the office."

After she took my number and told me that she would pass on the message, I hung up with the hope that he would call me as soon as possible.

Well, that worked out all right. If only the rest of my plan worked just as smoothly.

Chapter 7

After taking a hot shower, I looked over my agenda and realized that I had a lot of work to do, so I headed over to my office. Between the church's Founders Day program, all the organizations that I was involved with, and this other bull that had just come up, I felt like I was about to lose it. I just hoped that Cornell hurried and called me. I felt like my life could get out of control with this little indiscretion. I mean, how would I explain this to my congregation?

I also felt bad that this was a young man who had once attended this church with his grandmother. But for the past few years he had been a total mess. He couldn't stay out of trouble if he tried. Thanks to Monica, I could keep up with what was going on. I just hoped I could persuade him to take care of Grace for me. The last time I saw him, he spoke to me like I was just another person from the street. That young man had no respect for anyone. But he did tell me that he would do almost anything for the right price. I hoped this was still true.

Shoot, I had thought I would have the church to myself today. I had forgotten that today Tyerra Williams was scheduled to come in and do the Sunday bulletins. I could hear her popping her gum all the way down the hallway. Tyerra was a good girl. She was the oldest child of Deacon Tyrone and Sister Sharon Williams. She had six siblings, and she had just started classes over at the junior college. I let her work with the regular church secretary to make extra money. The Williams could definitely use all the help that they could get. Deacon Williams worked at the foundry, and Sister Williams had her hands full raising all those children of theirs.

Tyerra loved music. She had her Kirk Franklin CD playing on full blast. As I passed the secretary's office, I could see that she was busy working on the computer.

"Good morning, Sister Tyerra," I said, sticking my head in the door.

"Oh, Pastor Harris!" she gasped, holding her chest. "I didn't know anyone else was here! You scared me." She giggled. "I'll turn this music down right now." She spun around in her chair to turn the volume down on her portable CD player. "Now that's better. I was just working on the bulletins for Sunday." She smiled and turned back to her work at the computer.

I hesitated and watched her work for a few seconds.

"Can I get you a cup of coffee or something?" she asked, never looking up from her work.

"No, thank you," I said. "You just go right on doing what you are doing. I can get myself whatever I need. How are your classes coming along?"

"I'm doing all right, I guess." She stopped keying in information to smile up at me.

I took notice of how deep her dimples creased her cherub-like face.

"Biology is kind of hard, though," she went on to say.

"Good, good," I returned, half interested. "I have always known that you were a very smart young lady."

Her dimples were replaced by a confused expression. A few seconds passed before I realized that I wasn't listening to her anymore.

"I had better get to my office," I said, embarrassed, and quickly left the secretary's office. I couldn't help but think, *Man, that Tyerra is getting attractive. And she has a nice pair of legs for a girl her age.* Then I thought about the deacon and how he was about his family. They might not have much money, but they were a very close family. *I don't think I want to play on that playground,* I thought and laugh to myself as I unlock my office door. I hoped that crazy Cornell called me soon.

Chapter 8

Another day had gone to waste, and I needed to solve this problem so that I could get back on track with the church. I was getting hungry, so I turned out the light in my office and headed home.

Walking toward the parsonage, I could see that Teri had what seemed like every light in the house on. The television greeted me as I walked through the side door, so I turned the volume down.

"Oh, hey, dear," Teri yelled from the kitchen. I headed toward the kitchen and found her on her knees, washing the floor, with her favorite black scarf tied around her head like she was some old housemaid.

"I see you're cleaning again," I commented, a little irritated. "Why must you get down on the floor like some common maid? Why on earth do you have to wear that rag on your head like that? I have told you too many times that I can pay someone to clean this house."

She didn't respond. She only stopped cleaning for a moment, sighed heavily, and then went right back to what she was doing.

"It's just that I don't like to see my wife scrubbing floors, even if they are her own floors," I told her.

"Look, Randall." She paused and looked up from what she was doing. "We have had this discussion several times. This is my house, my home, and no one can or will clean it the way that I can." She rose, removed her rubber gloves, and threw them into the sink. "Please give it a break." She turned and left me standing alone in the kitchen to contemplate what she had said.

"Look, honey." I followed behind her. "I just want to make it easier on you. I'm sure that we would much rather be doing other things."

"We? When was the last time *we* did anything?" she shot back. "We . . . Please, you make me laugh."

"Teri, I'm not trying to start an argument with you, baby. I was just saying—"

"Don't say anything," she interrupted, "because I love cleaning my house. It relaxes me, and I enjoy it. I'm going to be the only woman who will do it. Okay?" She enunciated each word to drive home her point. "Now, if you don't mind, we can leave this particular subject alone."

"All right," I said, throwing my hands up in surrender. "You win. I hate it when we disagree, anyway. A pastor and his beautiful wife should never have to disagree, you know?"

"Well, a man and a woman will," she returned. "Why don't you get out of those clothes and take a quick shower while I fix you something to eat?"

"That's all right. I had a big lunch," I lied. "I'm not hungry."

Following me into the bedroom, she started straightening up a bit before she said, "Honey, I've noticed that you haven't been eating very well lately." With a puzzled look on her face, she continued, "Is my cooking that bad? You have never complained." She had to be joking.

I couldn't help but laugh. "You are so sensitive," I said, shaking my head at that ridiculous question. Yet I saw that she still had a concerned look on her face. I put my hands on her shoulders. "Look, I'm just tired, is all. With all that is going on over at the church and all my meetings and so on . . . And I told you that I had a big lunch today. Anyway, I can afford to lose a few pounds, can't I?"

She smiled warmly and hugged me around my waist. "Reverend Randall Harris, I will love you at any size."

"A shower does sound good, though," I said, winking, "especially if we take one together."

"You are a nut, Randall." She laughed.

"That's Reverend Randall to you, young lady." We laughed together.

"You go on and take your shower, Reverend. I have a lot to do."

"Come on, Teri," I whined like a little child. I took her by the hand. "Come on. Let's take a shower together first."

"Together, huh?"

I wouldn't let her finish her statement before I removed that ugly mammy scarf from her hair. Then I pulled the red T-shirt over her head. Her hazel eyes seemed to glisten under the bedroom lights. I tasted her butter-pecan skin with my tongue.

"Mmmm," I moaned. "You taste so good to me, baby."

"I've been sweating, Randall," she whispered.

"Oh yeah? But you taste so good," I said as I took a step back to examine her breasts. She had on one of her black lace numbers that drove me absolutely crazy. "My goodness, girl. You are so fine," I said as I slipped my right hand behind her back to unhook her bra, which I let fall to the floor as her breasts danced to her heavy breathing. I began to kiss them gently. I felt her nipples harden against my lips. "I may not make it to the shower," I whispered as I worked myself up to her lips and began to unfasten her jeans.

When the jeans fell, I noticed that she had on the panties that matched her bra. Now I knew that I wouldn't make it to the shower. I laid her on the bed, and she tried to remove the comforter so as not to mess it up. I got frustrated and snatched the thing off of the bed and tossed it on the floor.

"I just want to look at you," I said as I started to remove my clothes. Lying next to her, I looked deep into her eyes. They were so sensual, so beautiful. "Teri, you are my life," I whispered, rubbing my finger across her bottom lip. "I want you to know that." I felt a twinge of guilt as I thought about all the things that I had done. "I don't care what someone may say or what you may hear, I need for you to know that. I don't know what I would do if I were to ever lose you." I lost control of my voice, and it started to crack. "I swear, I just don't know."

"Shh," she said. "You never have to worry about that. I made a commitment to you and a promise before God." Her words were comforting to me. "I plan on keeping that promise, Randall." She stared back into my eyes.

"I just want you to know that no matter what happens, Teri, I love you from the bottom of my heart, and I always will. Please remember that."

"I know this, darling. I know that you love me," she said softly. "Now make love to me."

I sometimes wondered why I had to push things to the limit. Why did I do some of the things that I did? Why did I put everything that I had worked so hard to build in jeopardy? I loved my wife; she was my match in every way. I loved the way she looked, the way she walked, the way she talked, her style of dress. She was my equal, my soul mate. So why did I always have to go to the edge?

When I thought back to the apartment that we moved into when we first got married, I remembered that the living room and dining room area and the kitchen were cramped and stuffy, although we spent the majority of our time in the bedroom with the remote control. We ate, conversed, and made love all in the same room. I guess we did have plenty of good memories of that place. When I was called to Unity, we were both too happy to bid that place farewell.

Our home today was spacious, with three bedrooms and two and a half bathrooms. Our large living room had cream carpeting and a marble fireplace to match. The sofa, love seat, and chair went beautifully with the matching ivory, marble, and glass tables trimmed in eighteen-karat gold. Teri had ordered the gold mirror above the fireplace, and it had come all the way from South Africa.

My favorite room was on the other side of the living room. The den, or blue room, as we called it, had sky-blue carpeting and a cherrywood fireplace. The plush sofa, love seat, and chaise lounge were very comfortable. I loved to lie in the chaise with the remote control in hand, watching our sixty-two-inch plasma TV.

Her favorite room was the kitchen. It was massive, with white cabinets and sky-blue countertops. The kitchen island stood in the middle of the room, and the black and stainless-steel appliances made everything look so nice.

The master bedroom had two walk-in closets, one for me and one for her. Teri decorated this room in bright, vibrant colors: emerald green, sapphire blue, and fuchsia. The master bathroom, which was connected to the bedroom, had the same color scheme and a black toilet, his and her sinks, and a spa tub built right into the floor. This was my favorite place to relax and meditate.

I felt a nervousness down in the pit of my stomach when I thought that I could lose it all on account of my selfishness. I couldn't lose it all, and, most importantly, I couldn't lose Teri.

Chapter 9

Back-to-back meetings this morning were keeping me all tied up, and still I hadn't heard a word from that prison-bound thug Cornell. It was difficult for me to keep my mind on business. After my morning meeting, I headed over to the church.

Sister Betty Gary, the church secretary, was there working in her office. I could tell that Sister Gary was a woman who, in her day, might have turned a lot of heads. But the poor woman failed to realize that her days were over. She still had pretty nice legs, but her hips were spreading like the Red Sea. Her butt jiggled wildly, like a bowl full of Jell-O, because she stomped like she was killing roaches when she walked. And that was a bit too much for me. Her large breasts looked as if they were angry with one another and wanted to take refuge southward. And at her age she still insisted on wearing the tightest dresses and skirts. She also wore her hair weaved a foot high on her head, like these young girls, which made her giraffe neck look even longer than it was, my goodness.

The poor woman had five children at home, five children who all looked completely different from one another. I would never forget the Easter Sunday she lined them up in front of me and asked me if I thought they were the most beautiful kids I had ever laid eyes on. All I could think was that a monkey's mama thought her babies were cute. I immediately felt bad about what I was thinking, but they honestly looked like a crew of refugees in their cheap suits and dresses.

I also remembered a conversation we had had one day some time ago. She often complained about having man trouble. I told her I felt that maybe she needed to find an older, more settled man, one who wouldn't mind those bad kids of hers. Well, I didn't tell her that I thought her kids were bad, although everyone else did.

She had the nerve to tell me that she was not attracted to older men and that young men turned her on. Ump, ump, ump. Somebody really needed to sit down with this woman and have a good talk with her. Somebody needed to tell her the truth.

"Good morning, Pastor," she sang as I walk past her office.

"Good morning to you, Sister Gary." I pretended to be upbeat. "How are you?"

"I'm blessed, Pastor. You know me," she sang.

"I see that." I also saw that she was wearing that gray rayon dress that she thought she looked so good in. And her brightly painted toes were falling out of the sandals that she was wearing and were touching the floor.

"You look nice today," I said, forcing myself to lie.

"I just felt like dressing up today." She smiled.

"I see." I cleared my throat. "Well, you continue to enjoy your day."

"You do the same, Pastor," she said to my back as I turned and left her office.

I was surprised at the amount of work I got through today. I was starting to put some things away when the phone rang. *Maybe it's Cornell,* I thought.

Sister Gary picked it up in her office, and a few seconds later she knocked on my door.

"Pastor, Sister Sandra Cummings is on the phone, wanting to speak with you, and she seems to be pretty upset."

Taking a deep breath, I walked over to my desk. "Thank you, Sister Gary. I'll take the call now."

"Yes, this is Pastor Harris," I said into the receiver.

"Hello, Pastor," said a very upset voice. I could tell that she had been crying.

"What is it, Sister?" I asked, concerned.

"Pastor, things are all messed up! The police just left my house, and they took Malik to jail. They said something about him selling drugs. I know they are going to send him to prison this time," she said before blowing her nose in my ear and breaking down into sobs. "I don't know what I am going to do. He is all I got. I ain't got nobody else."

I gave her some time to compose herself.

"I just don't know. I have given that boy everything. I have always worked my tail off for him, when his no-good father wouldn't have anything to do with him. If they send him to prison, I don't know." She broke down once more.

"Sister Cummings," I said, "please try to calm yourself down. Try to take some deep breaths and relax. You can't afford to get yourself all worked up. Have you taken your high blood pressure medication today?"

"Yes." She blew her nose even harder in my ear this time.

"Where did they take him? Do you know?"

"Pastor, they just came into my house, and then they yelled at me and took my son," she replied, starting up again. "They tore my house apart and looked down on me like I was piece of garbage."

"I see. . . . Well, Sister, I insist that you lie down and relax. I will go downtown and try to find out what is going on for you."

"God bless you, Pastor. I really do hate to bother you like this, but I just didn't know what else to do. I'm still trying to pay off the lawyers from his last run-in with the law."

"I will call you as soon as I find out what is going on," I assured her before hanging up. Rubbing my forehead, I look up to see that Sister Gary was still standing in the doorway, taking everything in.

"I see that her son is in some kind of trouble again," she commented.

"Sister Betty, it is not nice to listen in on personal conversations," I scolded her.

"Oh, I wasn't," she quickly returned. "I just came in to tell you something. . . . I just forgot what it was." She rubbed her hands together.

I could see that she was embarrassed. "Oh, is that right?" I cut an eye at her.

"If I remember what it is, I'll leave you a note, since I see that you are going out," she blurted before turning to go back to her office.

"You do that," I couldn't help saying. She had some nerve.

When I got downtown, I had to wait nearly an hour to speak to someone. I was relieved when my old friend Detective Mike Riley came up to me. Mike had been on the police force for going on eighteen years now.

"Reverend Harris, what can I do for you?" He greeted me with an extended hand.

"Good evening, Mike. What I am here about is the Cummings kid. His mother is a faithful member of my congregation. She called the church, very upset, saying that he was picked up today and that it had something to do with him selling drugs."

"Come on into my office and have a seat," he said, directing the way with his hand.

Mike was a cop who came from a long line of cops. His father was a cop, and his father's father was a cop. But ole Mike was able to make it to detective.

Wanting to carry on the family legacy, Mike was a man who was never satisfied. He had a young Barbie doll wife at home, whom he loved to show off and take on luxury vacations and shopping sprees. He once explained to me that in order to keep his Barbie doll happy, he had to make more money than a detective's salary would allow. The word on the streets was that if you were in trouble, talk to Riley. He had put himself in some pretty shaky situations with some of the blacks, Latinos, and others on the wrong side of the law.

He knew that I knew some things about him. And he knew some things about me. We had found ourselves sometimes dealing with the same people.

Picking up a file from a stack on his desk, he opened it up.

"Well, Reverend, this is a pretty clear-cut case. We have that kid on film selling crack right out in the open. It hasn't made it to the DA's office yet, but it's an open-and-shut case."

"I figured that," I said, sitting back in my chair. "He is a piece of work. But is there something you can do this time as a favor to me?"

Placing both hands on the back of his head and making an odd face that I could not read, he finally let out a sigh. "This kid has a pretty good sheet going for him, you know?"

I nod my head in agreement.

"How many chances do you give someone like this? He is going to end up throwing his life away, anyway." He threw his hands up in the air to help make his point.

Lowering my voice, I moved in closer to him. "Mike, this is going to kill his poor mother. For her sake, please, can you help me out? Look, let's say we change the charges to possession or something like that. Lock him up in the county for a few months. What do you say? Huh? Just don't send him to prison."

Shaking his head, he replied that he didn't know about this one. "You already owe me, or do I have to remind you?" he whispered back. "Do you remember the night I had to tell your wife that you were having car trouble? The night that you couldn't seem to find your way home." He raised his eyebrows.

"Do you Irish ever forget anything?" I asked jokingly to ease the tension.

"No, and don't you forget it." He finally smiled back. "Okay, I'll see what I can do, but I promise you, Reverend, this is the last time that I'm going to do anything for this piece of crap. He is going to end up dead or in the pen sooner or later, anyway."

"Understood," I responded, relieved. I rose to shake his hand. "I really do appreciate this."

"I mean it. This is the last time," he repeated.

"I know, Mike! I know!" I was turning to leave his office when I said, "I'll keep in touch, buddy."

"For my sake, don't," he replied.

We both laughed and then I made my way through the police station and out the front door.

When I reached the Cummings's house, I saw right away that Sister Cummings hadn't done any of the things that I had asked her to do. She was sitting on her front porch, rocking back and forth and waiting for any word on that son of hers. I parked and got out of my car.

"Come on in the house, Sister Cummings," I urged. She got up and followed me inside. Pointing to her couch, I asked her to take a seat. I was searching my head for the right words to sugarcoat the situation when she interrupted my thoughts.

"Sorry about the mess, Pastor. It's just that I've been so worried about Malik."

"Yeah, I'm sure," I said under my breath. I had heard that she had always kept a filthy house. The flies were coming through a huge hole in the screen, and the carpet was so dirty that, I swear, you could plant seeds and watch them grow. Her off-white walls were greasy, clothes and papers were all over the place, and the house had a moldy smell, which she tried to hold back with mothballs. I didn't know which was worse.

"Well, Sister Cummings," I began as she stared me dead in the eye. "I spoke with someone downtown—"

"Did you get to see Malik?" she asked, interrupting me again.

"No, Sister, I didn't," I told her, and she looked down at the floor as I guided her to the stained green couch that sat against an even more grease stained wall. "But I think I talked them into reducing his charges. He will have to spend some time in county, but the good news is that he will not be going to prison."

"Oh no." She started to cry.

"Look, Sister Cummings," I said, a bit irritated at how she was carrying on, "they have got that boy selling dope on tape. I think spending some time in county will give him the time to figure out which way he wants to go. It will only be a few months, anyway. You can still go visit him if you want. At least he is not getting sent upstate. Now look at this as the blessing that it is."

She wiped her face with a towel. "You're right, Pastor. Thank you for everything. I mean that." She tried to smile.

Feeling a little bad now for snapping at her, I took her hand in mine and returned the smile. "You don't have to thank me. I'm just glad I could do something. Now please promise me that you will take care of yourself, and while you are on your knees praying, I want you to pray that

God will change the heart, mind, and attitude of your son. He has to change, and you know this. If he doesn't, this is going to continue to happen. Do you understand what I'm saying to you?"

She closed her tearful eyes and slowly nodded her head.

I assured her that things were going to work themselves out and gave her hand a squeeze as I got up to leave.

"Will you tell Sister Harris that I said hello? And will you continue to pray for me and my boy, please?" Her eyes filled with sadness.

"I sure will, Sister," I told her as I reached for the doorknob.

"And, Pastor," she said, getting up, "God bless you for all that you have done." She walked over to the front door, and I gave her a brief hug and let her go. "I wish I had some way of paying you back," she said. I wanted to tell her that she could get off her butt and clean her house, but that wasn't my place. And I could see the gratitude in her eyes.

"Just promise me that you will get some rest. That is all the thanks I need. Have a good night." I walked out and closed the door behind me.

When I got home, Teri had cooked supper. She noticed once again that I didn't have much of an appetite. I forced down my meal to please her. I filled her in on the day's events. She could only shake her head as she nibbled on her piece of garlic toast. After we ate, I grabbed the newspaper and went to the blue room, while Teri grabbed one of her books and followed. The news in the paper could not hold my interest as I played over the day's events in my head. I was thankful to have people in high places who could help me when needed. Detective Riley was one of them. Now I just had to get this other burden off my shoulders and things would be all right. I sighed heavily, causing Teri to look over her book at me. I was so glad that she didn't say anything. I did not feel like talking.

Chapter 10

"Honey, we are having another book club meeting tonight," Teri informed me.

"And what is that supposed to mean?" I asked.

"I thought I told you that. Please don't tell me that I forgot to tell you," she said as she searched her memory. "There were two scheduled this month. I could have sworn that I told you."

"It doesn't matter," I told her. "I'm sure I can find something to do to keep out of your way. How long is this little meeting supposed to last, anyway?" Only half interested, I poked at my eggs with my fork.

"Randall, this is your home also, and it is big enough for the both of us. What are you trying to say?"

"Nothing." I shoved a link sausage in my mouth. "Can I have some more coffee, please?" I pushed my cup across the island toward her.

"Honey," she said as she poured me a second cup, "I was thinking about going to Chicago to visit my family. You know I haven't been home in about five years now. If you don't want to go, I can go home alone."

I didn't say a word, so she raised her voice.

"Randall, I want to go home. I want to see Mama and Daddy."

Placing my cup on the island, I turned to look at her. "So what are you saying, Teri?"

"I'm saying that I want to see my parents. I miss them," she pleaded.

"So you want me to just up and forget all about the business of the church all because you are a little homesick?"

"No, Randall, you don't have to do anything. I do know my way home."

"I see. Then you're saying that you want to leave me here alone while I let you drive all over the United States?"

Choosing not to answer me, she turned to finish up the breakfast dishes.

"What's the matter with you now? Are you unhappy or something?"

"Why do I have to be unhappy just because I want to go home?" she snapped at me. "Tell me, why do I have to go through this just because I want to see my parents and my sisters? Why is it so hard for you to understand that? Huh? And why are you always questioning my happiness?"

I got up to leave the island, not wanting to get into an argument.

"See? You always walk away when I want to talk about something that you don't want to discuss. And another thing, whether you agree or not, Randall, I am going home to see my family," she informed me.

Stopping dead in my tracks, without turning around to face her, I said as calmly as I could, "Well, if you leave this house without my approval, you had better make it permanent." Then I walked out of the kitchen.

"Well, the choice is yours to make," she told me just as calmly.

When I got in the bedroom and thought about this thing for a while, I came to the conclusion that maybe I was being unreasonable. But Teri was my wife, and I needed her here with me. I wanted to take her places, but the church just kept me entirely too busy. Or maybe it was my guilt getting the best of me. Maybe it was just that

I didn't want her out of my sight because of the things that I did. She was beautiful, and I knew that other men saw this.

I decided to soak in the spa tub for a while before going out today. It was the best way to clear my mind when I was faced with difficult decisions. Visiting her parents for a while wouldn't be so bad. I was sure that I could get one of my associate ministers to handle the services until I got back. Or maybe it would be a good idea to let her go alone. I figured we could use a break from each other. It might do us both some good. She had spoiled me so; she even had my clothes laid out for me when I stepped out of the tub. Yeah, she had spoiled me rotten. She was too good to me, and I needed to straighten this mess out before I left the house this morning.

When I had dressed, I stepped into the kitchen, but I didn't see her. I checked the living room and the blue room, but she was nowhere to be found. My heart started to pound. I hoped that I didn't make her mad enough to leave without saying anything. She let me know every time she left the house. Passing the kitchen window, I saw that she was sitting outside on the patio. I closed my eyes and exhaled. I slowly walked toward the patio to spy on her as she sat on the chaise. The patio was L-shaped, so we could go out on it from the kitchen or the blue room. I was ashamed of myself for the way that I had carried on at breakfast, so I figured I would stand there for a few minutes, that is, until I saw just how terribly sad she was.

"Teri," I said softly. She didn't respond, so I opened the sliding door. "Sweetheart," I called out, waiting for a response. There was none. "Sweetheart, I'm so sorry for being such a butt hole. I know I can be stubborn and unreasonable sometimes. I can be so close-minded when it comes to you."

When I said this, she looked up at me, confused and still sad.

"I promise to make it up to you, dear. I promise." I stepped outside and sat on the chaise next to her. Then I took her hands in mine and looked into her hazel jewels. "I'm so sorry, honey. You know you can go and see your parents. I have been under so much stress lately that I acted like a complete idiot."

"Can we both go?" she asked, finally breaking her silence, the sadness still in her eyes.

"We are going to sit down tonight and talk about this rationally, okay?" I assured her. "I owe you that. Please forgive me for acting like such a child. As soon as your book club leaves tonight, we can sit down and talk about it, okay?"

"Okay," she said, finally giving me a warm smile.

This made me feel much better. "You are so beautiful, Teri. I love you." I gently kissed her top lip. "I'm going over to the office. I have a couple of meetings today. So it looks like I'll be out of your way, after all." I laughed.

"I'll see you this evening, Randall." She smiled.

I left for the office, leaving her resting on the chaise and enjoying the morning sun. It broke my heart to see my wife in such a state. But if I didn't take care of this problem, she would have many sad days ahead of her.

Chapter 11

As I left my first meeting of the day at the Boys and Girls Club, my cell phone rang. I didn't like to answer calls when I didn't recognize the number, but as a pastor, I felt obligated to do so.

"Hello, Cat Daddy," said a sexy voice through the receiver.

"Banks?" I said, surprised. "Is this you?"

"Of course it's me. Who else calls you Cat Daddy?"

"No one," I hurriedly answered her. "That name is only for you, baby."

"You just make sure that it stays that way, Mister," she teased. "So . . . would my Cat Daddy like to get his tongue a little wet tonight? Your kitty has been purring for you."

"Has it?" was all I could manage to get out. I was growing excited, just thinking about my girl Shaletta.

"It's been purring for you for a long time, and it needs its Cat Daddy," she moaned into the phone.

Shaletta Banks could make any man weak in the knees, and mine were about to collapse. Her dear ole mother had raised her to use her physical attributes to get the things she wanted. Her mother had also taught her that men were weak and were to be taken advantage of. I didn't agree, but her mother had taught her well. Shaletta could make a career out of men if she wanted to. And if she decided to do just that, she would have a pretty nice life, with a penthouse on Park Avenue and a mansion in the hills.

Shaletta was gorgeous. A caramel-colored beauty who looked like she had a hair and makeup team at her disposal. I had never caught her with a hair out of place, a nail chipped, or smudges in her makeup. She was always well put together from head to toe. Well . . . that is, if one could see around her somewhat large nose. I guessed it was a part of her ancestry, and some might even think that it was cute. Me, I could do without it. I tried to concentrate on her other traits. Like the fact that she had doe-shaped eyes that were very sensuous. And her hair looked like it was cut by a professional surgical team. I loved the way she maintained her long, manicured acrylic nails, which just drove me crazy when she ran them over certain parts of my body.

Now, the difference between Shaletta and the other women I had relationships with was that I could satisfy her orally. This was why she called me Cat Daddy. Just listening to her say my name made my mouth water.

"So what did I do to deserve this call?" I asked, trying not to sound too desperate.

"Well, I'm in town for a couple of days, and you know I couldn't leave without seeing you," she cooed into the phone, making my toes curl in my shoes.

"Oh yeah . . ." I was becoming tongue-tied again.

"You know what I mean."

"No. Tell me what you mean."

"Oh, you know how I feel about you, Cat Daddy."

"I just like to hear it sometimes."

"I have a whole lot to say if I can see you while I'm in town."

"Then I may just have to take you up on it." I tried my best to sound witty.

"I promise to make it worth your while," she said, still cooing and driving me crazy.

"I'm sure you will, Shaletta. Where are you?"

"I'm in the Royal Suite at the Bedlington Hotel."

"I know where that is," I told her. "I can be there around six this evening, after my last meeting."

"I'll be waiting for you, Cat Daddy," she moaned.

A shiver ran down my spine as I pressed the end button on my phone. Man, that girl was a trip. Well, I needed to be out of Teri's hair, anyway, this evening. Plus, I could not pass up a chance to be with my sweet, sweet Shaletta Banks. There was no telling when I would get a chance to see her again.

Chapter 12

Riding the elevator up to the Royal Suite of the five-star Bedlington Hotel, our little hide away on the outskirts of town I was as intrigued as a fat man in the bakery aisle of a grocery store. I had to admit that every encounter with Shaletta was an adventure. I could smell her favorite Cool Water incense the instant that I stepped off the elevator. *Man, that smells good,* I thought. I could hear music softly playing as I approached the suite. She had left the door ajar.

"Knock, knock," I said as I pushed the door open wider.

"Come on in here, Cat Daddy," she drawled in her Southern accent. She was sitting on the couch in a purple negligee, her long legs crossed and a slit running all the way up her left leg. "You are always right on time, aren't you?" she cooed as I walk over to her side of the room.

"You know you shouldn't leave your door open like that," I scolded her. "I could have been anyone."

Slowly uncrossing her legs, she stood to greet me. "But you aren't just anyone, are you, Cat Daddy?" She put her arms around my neck and placed wet kisses on my lips. "I've missed you."

"I've missed you too, Shaletta."

"I want you to show me just how much you've missed me," she whispered as she took my earlobe into her mouth. "Can't you hear my kitty purring?"

"Yes," I answered, getting more aroused from her warm, wet tongue going in and out of my ear. "Yes, yes, I hear it purring."

"It's purring for its Cat Daddy," she whispered. Stepping back to take a good look at me, she added, "You feel a little tense. What's the matter?"

I couldn't say anything. I remained silent.

"Come on over to the bed and let me give you a massage."

I still couldn't find any words as she led me to the bed like I was a man in a trance. Never taking her eyes away from mine, she bent down on the floor in front of me and removed my shoes and socks. Rising to sit next to me on the bed, she removed the cuff links from my shirt. Then she loosened my tie and raised it over my head. She slowly unbuttoned my shirt, then gestured for me to stand and unfastened my belt and pants. I complied like an obedient child.

"I see you have been taking good care of yourself," she whispered as she swallowed my right lobe once more and wet it with her tongue.

Words still had not found their way to my mouth.

Next, she gestured for me to lie down on the bed, on my stomach. She dimmed the lights to give the room a mellow glow, then lit candles around the whole room. I became more relaxed than I had been in a long while as I breathed in the sensual aroma of the incense. I watched the flame dance erotically on a particular candle.

I closed my eyes as she massaged my feet and slowly moved up to my calves. She worked on my thighs as if she were kneading bread, and it felt good. Then she straddled my back and placed hot kisses all over my shoulders.

"I just want you to relax and feel good," she said between kisses.

Stretching out my arms, she began to massage my fingers, then my hands, my arms, and my shoulders. As she continued down my back, I couldn't believe how she had almost made me forget about all the problems that were waiting for me on the other side of the door.

"Turn over for me," she ordered. "I want you totally relaxed for this."

Again, I obeyed like a child would his mother. I did what she wanted me to do. She swirled her hot tongue around my nipples, and I had to fight hard to maintain my composure. The hot steam from her nostrils was driving me crazy. She moved down to my navel, and my stomach began to jump.

"Oh, my goodness," I moaned. "My, my, my." Twirling her tongue around and around, I wanted to ask her to stop. "Oh my," I continued to moan, but she just would not let up. "I can't take any more of this," I strained to tell her.

She ignored me and continued with her new art form. I could not contain it any longer. Before I knew it, I was lying on the bed, unable to move a muscle. Slowly, she slithered up next to me, taking my lips into her mouth.

"How did you like that?" she asked as she continued to work on my face with her mouth.

I declare, that woman had the energy of a lioness.

"I loved it," I responded weakly, out of breath. "Where did that come from?"

"Oh, just a little something . . . something that I have been perfecting just for you," she told me.

And I believed that just as surely as I believed there was a big, fat white man in a red suit who drove a sleigh through the sky every year, delivering toys around the world.

"I just wanted to make you feel good, because you have made me feel so good many, many times."

"Who have you been perfecting your skills on?" I asked, surprised to find myself a little jealous.

"Why do you feel like I have to be practicing on anyone?" She raised a brow. "Why couldn't I have just used my imagination?"

"Well, you have one heck of an imagination."

"Only when it comes to you, Cat Daddy," she squealed. "You seem to bring out the freak in me."

After we lay there for a while, catching up on the latest, I was ready to please my kitty, and I told her this. She squealed once more as I slid my tongue past her breasts. I could tell right away that they were pleased. She curled her long legs over my shoulders as I worked my way down to her navel.

"My goodness," I reported to her.

"I told you that I've missed you," she panted.

"My goodness, Shaletta Banks, my goodness."

Chapter 13

I got home later than I had planned, so I thought that Teri would be fast asleep. She wasn't. I bet she'd stayed up because I had promised her we would talk about her trip. Trying my best to look composed, I asked her as I walked in the house, "So how did the book club meeting go tonight?"

"It was nice," she told me. "We discussed the book by Mary Monroe entitled *The Upper Room*." She was still excited about it, I guessed. She tended to get all caught up in that reading group. A bunch of women sitting around, discussing nothing. You would think that they had better things to do.

"Oh, a religious book?" I asked, trying to sound interested.

"No, sweetie, it's not a religious book." She laughed.

"I know you aren't reading any of those dirty books in the parsonage, are you?" I joked.

She only laughed me off as she stretched and rose to pick up the leftover finger foods, paper plates, cups, napkins, and other items from the meeting.

"You know we can't have that sort of stuff lying around," I said, continuing to joke. "At least not out in the open. What is there to eat? I'm hungry."

"I bought you a chicken dinner from Annie Mae's, because I knew you wouldn't be interested in what we were having. What you usually refer to as sadiddy foods" she laughed to herself.

She warmed up my meal and placed it on the table as we continued to joke with one another.

"Thank you," I told her. "After I eat and take a shower, we can finish the discussion that we started this morning."

"Randall, I'm in such a good mood from the meeting that I don't think I want to finish the discussion."

"Teri . . . it's just that I realize how selfish I am when it comes to you. How stupid I can be."

She sat down in the chair next to me with the biggest smile on her face. "Well, I see we are going to talk about this now." She took her finger and wiped chicken grease from my mouth.

"See? What am I going to do without you?" I said, trying to lighten the moment. I pushed my plate away and sat back in my chair when I notice that the expression on her face had turned serious. "It seems to me that you have something to say. Go ahead and tell me what's on your mind."

As I waited for a reply, I watched her and she looked as if she was deep in thought. "Randall," she began, "I am your wife, and I have tried my best to make and keep you happy—"

"You have done just that," I interrupted.

"Please let me finish." She held up her hand. "As your wife, I have gone where you've wanted me to go. From the beginning of our marriage, I have stood by every decision you've made. Decisions concerning the church, your career, and this house. What I'm saying, Randall, is that I have put my life on hold, and I've never complained. It's just that I feel when I ask you for a small favor, small compared to all the things you have asked me to do for you, sweetheart, I don't think you should get so upset. I went to college because I wanted a career. You and the few people I associate with from the church are the only friends I have in this town."

"Teri, let me interrupt for a second. I agree with you wholeheartedly. I have been thinking about this all day. I have been a fool. I guess all I have ever thought about was working hard and giving you the sort of life I thought you deserved. The sort of life you do deserve. But all the while doing this, I have neglected you. But I promise you tonight, Teri, that things are going to change. Now, I am going to be busy for the next couple of weeks, but I understand you want to go home and visit your family. In fact, I think it would be good for you to go alone. And when you get back, I think it will be a good idea for you to utilize your skills for the betterment of the community. You deserve to be complete and fulfilled."

"You truly feel this way, Randall?" she asked in amazement.

"Yes, I do. I believe you have a lot to offer this community, and I tell you, honey, seeing you so sad this morning tore me up. It got me to see just how unreasonable I was being. But you have to realize that some of this is your fault also."

"My fault? What do you mean, my fault?" I could tell she was taken aback.

"If you hadn't spoiled me so, then I wouldn't be such a big brat."

Her enchanting hazel eyes smiled at me. Captivated, I realized that I would never love anyone as much as I loved her.

Chapter 14

For the past few days Teri and I had been getting along just beautifully. We'd been laughing, talking, and having lots of fun, just like at the beginning of our relationship. I hadn't had much time to work on my sermon for the week, so I would just have to speak from the heart. It had always seemed to come together well when I had to do so in the past.

I was told that Mother Wiley was back in the hospital and that she was not doing very well at all. She was one of the oldest mothers of my congregation. For someone as quiet as she was, she was so full of wisdom and knowledge. I truly missed her when she was not in service. I'd have to send some special prayers up for her.

"Come on, honey. I don't want us to be late for Sunday school," I called out to Teri as I checked my suit one last time in the bedroom mirror.

"I'm ready," she said, hopping into the kitchen with one shoe on and the other in her hand.

I waited for her to finish putting the other shoe on and straighten her lavender suit, which I thought she looked magnificent in. "You look wonderful, darling," I told her.

"Thank you," she said, beaming. "So do you."

"Well, my queen, may I have the honor of escorting you to church this morning?" I held out my hand to her.

"Why, you most certainly may, my king." She giggled as she took my hand. We walked to church, laughing all the way, like two high school teenagers on a first date.

Sunday school went great, and so did the morning services. The Unity Choir was phenomenal. We were having dinner in the church hall to kick off Women's Annual Day. The sisters served a wonderful menu that consisted of fried and baked chicken, spiral ham, turkey and dressing, macaroni and cheese, turnips, mustard greens, green beans, potato salad, sweet potatoes, homemade dinner rolls, and a variety of desserts. I didn't really like to brag, but Unity had some of the best cooks in town. Okay, yes, I did like to brag.

After we blessed the food, I sat at the head table with Teri and a few of our friends, and we ate and had a great conversation. I enjoyed this time with my members, and we were having a really good time. That is, until Brother Dixon, Grace's father, walked by. I instantly lost my appetite. Brother Dixon was a tall, well-built man with broad shoulders and huge hands, I assumed from years of hard work at the steel plant. He was a somewhat good-looking man and had rich butterscotch skin. I knew that if he knew what was going on with Grace, he would take my head off with his bare hands.

"Good afternoon, Pastor Harris," he said, stopping at my table.

"Well, good afternoon to you, Brother Dixon." I tried to mask my discomfort. I shook his hand and asked, "How are things going for you?"

I noticed that he had a covered plate in his hand, which meant that he wasn't staying.

"I'm taking a plate home for Grace. She is a little under the weather today," he informed the table.

"Oh?" I said, trying to seem surprised. "Could it be a bug or something?"

"I'm not sure, Pastor. She has been a little distant lately. She is still grieving for her mother, I take it." He had a sad look on his face.

"Hopefully, she will come around soon, Brother Dixon. The church is still praying for the both of you." I wanted to comfort him with my words.

"Well, I won't hold you up, Pastor, Sister Harris." He nodded at my wife. "I better get this food home while it's still warm. Just keep us in your prayers," he mumbled before walking out of the church hall. He left me sitting at the table, feeling guilty and angry all at the same time.

This new dilemma that I had gotten myself into could lead me to lose the respect of everyone sitting at my table. And Teri . . . I didn't even want to think about what would happen between us. I sat quietly while our guests continued to converse and have a good time. I couldn't get the fact that Cornell Hollis hadn't called me yet. Shoot, he didn't have anything else to do. All he did was hang out in those streets.

Chapter 15

When Mother Wiley got up and around, maybe I would take Sister Gary to see her so that they could have a talk. If anyone could get her out of those tight dresses, I knew Mother Wiley could. I did love a good-fitting dress on a bomb body. That is, if, and only if, everything was in the right places. But I swear that something new stuck out on my secretary every week. And I couldn't take it any longer.

"Pastor, you have a call from Sister Grace Dixon," she said, interrupting my thoughts as I sat at my desk, staring out the window at the magnificent spread of flowers that had bloomed around the church. The sky was such a clear blue; there wasn't a cloud in sight. "I can take a message if you're busy," she offered.

"No, I'll take it, and thank you." Then, trying to find the words, any words to send her away from the church for a while, I asked her if she had any aspirins for a headache.

"No, sir, but I can pick you up a bottle. I'm about to run out and get some lunch." She hurried around my office.

"Good. That will be just fine," I said, relieved.

"I'll be gone for about forty-five minutes to an hour, if that's all right with you."

"That will be just fine," I repeated once more before she stormed out of my office like a tornado. Shaking my head and taking a deep breath, I picked up the receiver.

"Pastor Harris speaking."

"Hello. This is Grace," came a soft voice through the line.

"Yes, I know."

"My father is becoming suspicious and asking me all sorts of questions. It is really making me nervous about this whole thing."

"Oh," was all that I could muster up the nerve to say as I swallowed a big lump in my throat.

"I think this is a good time for me to talk to him about what's going on with me. I think he has a pretty good idea of what's up."

"Oh."

"I'm going to have to tell him who the father is."

"Okay, Grace. I understand."

"I don't think that you do. For some reason, you seem to feel as though I have all this time, and I don't."

"Can you give me until the end of the week?" I found myself begging with this girl, when I really didn't want to have to.

"Why? What is your big plan?" She was yelling in the phone at this point.

"Just do this for me, and everything will work out. I promise you."

I didn't know what else to say to her. I just wanted to stall for some more time. I needed for Cornell to call me ASAP.

"Look, you have made several promises to me that you did not keep. Now look at this big mess we've made. You came to me and told me that you wanted to help me through my mother's death. Well, you helped me, all right. You helped real well. My mother would be so proud of me right now. You lied to me, and you used me. You told me that you were my friend. You told me that I could come to you for anything. Now what? Some friend you turned out to be," I heard her mumble on the other end.

She went on. "Just as soon as you slept with me a few times, the telephone calls stopped. And when I could reach you, the conversations were short and abrupt. Now my life is turned upside down. I hope you know that you aren't the only one with something to lose. And after all this, you have the nerve to ask me to give you some more time. What do you have to give me, huh? More of your counseling sessions? More of your laying-on-the-hands sessions?" she asked sarcastically.

"Grace, try to remain calm about this. I can feel that you are getting upset."

"Spare me the drama, Pastor Harris. Like you care."

"Whether you believe me or not, Grace, I do care."

"I don't believe you," she said, blasting me through the phone line. "And I will tell you something else. I am not playing by your rules anymore. I have weighed the negatives and the positives in this matter. If worst comes to worst, all I have to do is join another church. In a few short weeks, my stomach will be growing, and I will have to explain it to everyone. The way that I see it, the sooner people find out about this whole thing, the sooner I can go on with my life."

"Grace," I said, jumping in, "I know you don't think too highly of me right now, but I am going to help you through this. All I ask is that you give me a chance. Give me a chance to talk to my wife about this, and then we can both talk to your father."

"Your *wife?*" I could tell by the inflection of her voice that she couldn't believe I had said that. "You are going to tell your wife?"

"Yes . . . I feel she should know before it gets out."

She laughed sarcastically, and I felt that this conversation was getting old pretty quick.

"Look, Grace . . . at the end of the week I will come to you, and together we can go to your father. I do care about this baby, and I care about you," I lied.

There was a long silence on the line.

"I will call you in a couple of days," I told her.

"Yeah, right," she said before hanging up the receiver in my ear.

"What in the heck have I gotten my butt into this time?" I caught myself saying out loud. What could I say to Teri about this situation? She would probably want to leave me, at least for a while. I couldn't lose Teri. Not like this. She had been my only real girlfriend, my only true love. I had not had any experience with any women before her.

I thought back to our wedding day. She was stunning, and I was the proudest groom in the world. I had wanted the traditional church wedding, but she wanted to get married in her mother's flower garden. She had on a white, formfitting, backless dress with a long train that flowed several feet. I had to admit that it couldn't have been more beautiful. The celery-green color of her bridesmaids' dresses blended in so well with the colors of the garden. With the sun just about to set, the garden was the perfect backdrop for our special day. The day that we looked into each other's eyes and promised before God and man to love each other forever. She was so breathtaking that day.

I remembered being so nervous when I took her hand from her father's. She just cried and cried into my black tuxedo, and I couldn't help but shed a few tears of my own. Our lives together were going to be perfect, I promised. I was going to be the pastor of a big church, and she its first lady. Her parents were also very happy, and she made me happy.

I couldn't imagine losing it all. I had better get off my butt and find that stupid thug Cornell. It didn't look like he was going to call me back, so I would have to go out and find him. I would just leave Sister Gary a note asking her to leave the aspirin on my desk and telling her that I would see her tomorrow. I scratched out a quick note, taped it to my door, and quickly rushed out of the church to my car.

Chapter 16

I was starting to get annoyed at the fact that I had been riding around and burning my gas for hours and hadn't found Cornell Hollis anywhere. Just when I was about to give up and go home, I saw him coming out of the liquor store on Lawrence and Seventy-Fifth Street. He and a couple of his thug buddies then walked down the street with wife beater T-shirts on and their jeans hanging half off their behinds. *Oh, my goodness,* was my first thought. I could see that Cornell had on a pair of Sean John jeans. He also had a do-rag on his head and Timberland work boots on. Like he had a job. Each of them had gold jewelry on—I mean, they were iced out—and they all looked like bad news.

I parked across the street after following them a couple of blocks. I watched as they walked, talked, laughed, and just hung out, wasting time in front of a run-down building. Wasting a lot of time doing nothing. My only thought at the time was, *My goodness, the cops are riding deep in this neighborhood today.* Every few seconds one would roll by. This was getting boring, so I finally decided to call him over.

"Hey, Cornell! Can I talk to you for a minute?" I yelled from my car.

"Who is that nigga?" I heard one of his friends say.

All of them were squinting their eyes and trying to make out who I was.

"Can I talk to you, man?" I rolled the glass down farther and stuck my head out the car window.

"If you want to talk to me, you bring your tail across this street to me and talk," he yelled back before he spit.

"Yeah, you come to us," yelled one of his friends, who looked more like a sea donkey, before breaking into laughter.

"Okay." I rolled my window up and stepped out of my car. I saw Cornell's expression automatically change, and then he broke into laughter.

"Ah, heck, naw. It's the preacher man," he said, and they all broke into laughter.

Laughing myself but not moving away from my car, I asked him, "Now can I speak to you?"

"About what? Don't you need to be out saving some souls or something like that? Don't you?" he asked again sarcastically, taking a drink from the bottle he held. Still laughing, he went on to say, "Nigga, you better be trying to save your own."

"Did your grandmother give you my message?"

"Yeah."

"Then why didn't you call me back?"

"What do you want with me, anyway?" He spit another plug of phlegm on the pavement.

"I just want to talk to you about something, is all." I was trying to remain calm at this point, because I could see that his boys were growing attached to my Cadillac.

"About what?" He had an angrier tone to his voice now. "Look, I'll catch y'all niggas later," I heard him tell his buddies. "Let me find out what this mark, this trick mofo wants with me." After a round of "aw-ights" and pounding fists, he pulled up his jeans slightly, looked both ways for traffic, and was on his way across the street to where I was waiting for him.

"Do you want to take a ride with me so that we can talk some business?" I asked him.

The smell of weed was all over him. "Yeah, and I got something that I need to talk to you about too, nigga," he stated.

"What do you have to speak with me about?" I was growing concerned.

"Hey, you came looking for me, aw-ight?" he snapped.

He opened the passenger door and got into my car as if it was his. We rode a few blocks, with him checking out the interior of my car, before he said anything else.

"So what's up, Preacher?"

"How are things going for you, Cornell?" I was trying to break the tension between us.

"Look, call me Cee. I hate my name. My crackhead mama named me after some old nigga that she assumed was my daddy. I don't know the muthasucka, so don't call me by his name. My boys don't know me by no Cornell, anyway."

"Fine then, Cee," I said. "How are things?"

"Not about ish. Now, what in the freak do you want?"

"Well, I was hoping that I could get you to do something for me, or I should say, a friend of mine."

Sitting up in his seat, he appeared to be surprised, irritated, or interested. "What do you want me to do?"

"We will get to that later. Now, have you found a job since you've been back home?"

"Heck, naw."

"Have you been looking?"

"Heck, yeah, but ain't nobody hiring no nigga fresh outta lockdown. Shoot, I need to make my money. I need to take care of my grandmama. Look, Preacher . . . what do you want with me?" He seemed to be growing restless.

"You use a lot of bad language, Corn. I mean Cee."

"Aw, heck, naw." He started laughing again. "Cut the freaking BS, preacher man, because I know all about your foul behind." He looked me square in the eyes.

"What do you mean?" was all my nervousness would let me ask. He had caught me a little off guard, and I didn't want him to know how uncomfortable I was.

"Heck, yeah." He continued to laugh as he checked me out from the corner of his eye. "When I was on lockdown, I used to talk with this young nigga named Trey. Trey was cool and everything. I just didn't trust the nigga. He was always in my grill, trying to scheme up on something. He used to like to brag too much about the things that he used to do on the street."

This was making me very uneasy, but I wasn't going to let Cee see this.

"He used to brag about how he always kept his pockets full. And he used to always talk about your foul behind," he went on. "How you used to spot him to make money. How you would put up the money, and he would work the streets and flip it for you. He also told me how you used to hang out at his uncle's club, in the VIP room. Yeah, he said that you was his nigga. That is, until the po-po tore his stuff up and took his black tail to jail. And to top it all off, he told me that your sorry butt was nowhere to be found."

I tried to think of something legitimate to say. "The police did come around, asking questions, all sorts of questions. I couldn't tell them anything," I said, hoping that it would help make Cee more at ease with me and my intentions.

"Trey said that he looked around for you in court and that you wouldn't even take the nigga's calls. Now, that's some BS, Preacher," he spat.

"I tried to tell Trey that they were asking around about him and things, but that boy was just too greedy. When he started making the big money, I couldn't tell that boy anything. He wouldn't listen to me at all."

"Yeah, that's Trey for you. But you could have taken the brotha's calls, Preacher. That was just jacked up."

"Trey just wasn't trying to listen to reason anymore, so I had to cut him loose."

"Well, I guess that sometimes you got to do what you got to do," he said, scratching the nappy hair that had grown on his chin and looking out the car window at the busy city streets. Looking at me again, he said, "Trey also told me that you used to pull plenty of women. He told me that those hoes loved your black behind." He started to laugh again.

"I don't know about all of that," I tried to say with a straight face.

Suddenly he stopped laughing and stared out the window again. "Well, now that you've wasted enough of my time and brought down my high, tell me, man, what do you want with me?"

"Well, Cee . . . I have a way that you can make some money. But this has to stay between the two of us."

He sat silently.

"I have got this friend," I continued, "who has gotten himself in a little trouble, I guess you can say."

"Oh yeah?"

"Yes. He is a married man, and he has gotten this young lady pregnant."

He looked at me as if I was crazy.

"It must be your sorry butt," he said after a few seconds and started laughing once more.

"No, no, it's not me at all. It's a friend of mine, who wants to remain secret."

"What am I supposed to do?"

"Well, he will pay you good money to find someone to—"

"Hey, man," he interrupted me. "I ain't killing no pregnant ho. You can let me out where you picked my black butt up at. Shoot, you trying to get a nigga locked up for life?" He put his hand on the door handle.

"No, no, no, it's not like that," I said, trying to calm him down. "He just wants someone to help her lose the baby—you know, maybe make her trip down some stairs or fall on her stomach. Something like that."

"You is tripping, or you are fricking crazy." He looked into my eyes to figure me out.

"So, Cee," I said, exhaling, "do you think that you can find someone to take care of this for him?"

"It depends on what a nigga gone pay. You know what I mean?"

"He is willing to pay between four hundred and six hundred dollars for a good, clean job."

"Heck, I beat a witch's butt for way less than that." He laughed once more. And it was getting on my nerves. "I've whipped a witch for free," he stated proudly. "Heck, I will do it for him. I need that kind of money. Who is the witch? Where does she live?" I could tell he was getting very excited, as his body had started rocking in the seat.

"Cee, now, you can't tell anybody about any of this, not even your boys. Is that clear?" I tried to drive home my point.

"Yeah," he answered. An irritated expression had crossed his face due to the fact that I was giving him orders.

"I'll call you tomorrow with all the information you'll need."

"For sho'! But my cell is turned off, and I may need to get your number to get in touch with you. I haven't been staying at my grandmama's house lately."

"That's funny. She told me that you were. And that you were in school."

"I still take care of my grandmama." His voice was lower, all the excitement drained from it.

I gave him my cell number. He looked at it like he was studying for a test. Then he shoved it deep into his jeans pocket.

"I'll call you tomorrow for sho'."

"And I will be waiting to hear from you."

With our business meeting taken care of, I gladly dropped him off in front of the building where I'd picked him up.

Chapter 17

Time was dragging as I sat around, waiting for Cornell—well, I beg your pardon, Cee—to call. I had given a lot of thought to what I would say to him. I didn't want him tracing Grace's pregnancy back to me. He had given me his word that he wouldn't talk, but a street thug's word didn't mean a thing unless you were one of them. And when it came to going to jail, they would sometimes turn on each other.

The only call that I had gotten so far today was from Monica's self-conscious butt, wanting to meet later in the week. I made up a big story about doing something with the church. I couldn't care less if she bought it or not. I had other things on my mind.

Teri and I had been getting along just wonderfully, and she was preparing for her trip to visit her parents. I would let her spend a few days with them, and then I would go there and spend a few days with my in-laws. I was sure Reverend Andrews would love for me to preach at his church again. He was getting old, and his small congregation always greeted me with a lot of love. It was late in the afternoon, and I was simply wasting time sitting around the office. I had better head on over to Annie Mae's. I was pretty sure the other ministers were already there, waiting for me.

Walking into the soul food restaurant, I could see that the group was there. As I walked over to the table, they all stood to greet me.

"Good afternoon, gentlemen," I said to everyone.

Soon we were all ready to get down to business.

"It's so good to have you here with us today, Reverend Evans," I said. "Last week we had two new ministers come on board. I'm sure that you have all had a chance to get acquainted with one another."

"Yes, we've all been sitting here talking and getting to know each other," he responded.

A very homely waitress strolled over to our table and placed glasses of ice water in front of each of us. "I'll be back fo' y'aw's orders in jest a few minutes," she said in a heavy country Southern drawl.

I looked up in time to notice that she had more space in her mouth than teeth. And the few teeth that she did have were discolored.

"Thank you," I said as I stared into her mouth. I was brought back to myself when I heard Sister Annie Mae barking out orders back in the kitchen. Reverend Cole commented that he had been back to the restaurant twice since I brought him last week. This made the whole table erupt in hearty laughter. He had such a serious look on his face when he told us this.

After the toothless waitress came and took our orders, we were able to talk business until she returned shortly thereafter, delivering our delicious meals. We sat discussing the latest business of the Ministers Alliance, and we were having such a great time that none of us realized how much time had passed. That was, until Sister Annie Mae slid over to our table in her ever-present black, fluffy house shoes.

"Good afternoon, everyone. I do trust that everything was satisfactory." She had the biggest smile on her face.

We all agreed that it was.

"Wonderful. Then, Pastor, I would like for you to meet somebody," she said. "Thea!" she yelled across the room, causing everyone in the restaurant to stop what they were doing to stare at her. The toothless woman walked over to our table.

"Pastor, this here is my cousin Thea," she stated proudly. "She just came up here from Mound Bayou, Mississippi. She came to help me run my restaurant."

"That's so nice," I said, trying not to stare into her mouth.

"She is going through a messy divorce, and I felt that she should come up here for a while to see if she likes it here. I'm bringing her to church Sunday. Who knows, she may just become a new member." She laughed to herself.

"That would be wonderful," I said. If she got her mouth fixed, she might not look half bad. "We welcome you, Sister Thea," I said to her. *Yeah, she does have nice eyes,* I thought. "How do you like our fair city so far?"

"Aw, Reverend, it's jest fine. I jest got to git used to it, is all." She held her head down out of shyness or shame.

"I'm sure you will, and I look forward to seeing you at church Sunday." I smiled, hoping to ease her nervousness.

"Thank yah," she returned, still looking down at the floor.

"Well, we got to get back to work. You know this place don't run by itself," Sister Annie Mae declared. She and her homely cousin walked back into the kitchen.

We got up, paid our bills, and said our good-byes.

Chapter 18

No more meetings today, I thought. *What a relief.* But I couldn't quite relax until I heard from Cee. I needed to see if this plan was feasible and if it would be carried out and handled in a well-thought-out manner. I had been second-guessing myself all day, wondering if in fact I had picked the right person to carry out the deed. I was becoming a little edgy. To waste time, I decided to call Teri to see what she was up to.

"Hello, darling," I said when she answered the phone. "How is my lovely wife this wonderful afternoon?"

As soon as she began to answer, my cell phone rang. It was a number that I did not recognize.

"Honey," I said, interrupting her, "I have a very important call that I must take. I will have to call you back."

Answering the cell phone, I could hear loud music in the background, so loud that I had to remove the phone from my ear several times.

"Yeah, this is Cee. Have you talked with your man yet?"

"Yes," I told him. "I spoke with him this morning, and he is very anxious to get this over with as soon as possible."

"So when can I meet your boy?"

"Well, um . . . he doesn't think that it would be a good idea for you two to meet. That's why he wanted me to set the whole thing up. You see, he is somebody with a lot to lose if this gets out. I also agree that the two of you shouldn't meet."

"Aw-ight, 'cause it don't matter to me if I meet ole boy or not. Man, I just want to get paid."

"I can meet you at the Burger King on Sixty-Seventh and King Drive in a half hour or so."

"That'll work." He told me that he wasn't very far from there, and hung up the phone without saying another word.

In less than twenty minutes, I was sitting in the Burger King parking lot, waiting for Cee to show up. After about another half hour or so Cee came walking up the street as if he didn't have a care in the world. The only difference in his appearance from yesterday was that he had a stocking cap on his head instead of that do-rag. He didn't look around to see if I was in the parking lot. I figured that he was high or drunk. I blew my horn to get his attention. He looked my way, grabbed his jeans on each side, so that they wouldn't fall off his butt, I assumed, and jogged to my car. He ran over to my side of the car, and out of breath, he bent down to ask me why I wasn't going inside.

"No thanks. I think it would be better if we spoke out here."

"Well, a nigga hungry. Can't you buy me a burger, a sandwich, or something? What kind of a businessman are you?" He seemed quite serious.

I pulled out a ten-dollar bill for him to buy something to eat. After all, I didn't want to get on his bad side this early in the game.

After a few minutes, he came strolling over to the car, eating a Whopper with one hand and holding a bag and large soda with the other. He walked over to the passenger door, climbed in, and then plopped down in the seat, wiping his mouth with the back of his hand. After burping with all that was in him, he finally sat back.

"Aw-ight, Preacher. What's up? How much your boy gonna pay me?" He started in on his second sandwich.

"He wants to know how much you would normally charge for a job like this one."

"If he's willing to pay up to six hundred dollars, I say that's cool."

"Six hundred dollars!" I said, not realizing that I had in fact offered that much. "Tell me what you plan on doing for that amount of money."

After stuffing what was left of his sandwich in his mouth, he said, "I don't want to hurt nobody too bad, because I ain't going back to jail for nobody. You hear me? Nobody. I figure I could probably scare her real bad, maybe rob her, ya know? Slap her around a little bit, ya know?"

I was becoming concerned about poor Grace at this point, but I knew it was too late for that, too late to turn back now. On the one hand, I wanted to speak with her. But I was afraid that I wouldn't be able to go through with this craziness if I did.

"I don't want you to hurt her too badly, either," I said, trying to convince him.

"Naw, the worst that I will do to her is that she will probably end up in the ER, maybe."

I was really starting to rethink this whole thing. "Maybe this isn't such a good idea," I said finally, after giving him some time to think about it.

"It's up to ole boy, you know," he said between slurps of soda. "If he can handle the baby mama drama, then it's on him."

"I just know for a fact that he doesn't want her to get hurt too badly. I don't think she deserves it, uh . . . but you know. I really don't know the young lady." I peered at him to see if he had noticed the slip of tongue.

"It's up to y'all. I need some money, and I don't mind slapping the hell out of some witch to get it, either."

"Cee, why do you use such horrible language?"

"What? Nigga, please."

"Do you talk like this in front of your grandmother?" Right away I could tell that I had hit a sore spot with him.

He stared at me real hard, as if he wanted to hit me. I turned to look out my window.

"My granny is my heart, man. As far as I'm concerned, she is the sweetest person on this whole darn messed-up earth. Now my mama, she can kiss my butt. All the whore ever thought about was getting high and lying up with some bum-ass niggas. She ain't never cared about me, my brother, or my grandmama. What she did care about was the welfare checks. My granny raised me, and she took care of me and my brother. She is the only person who I will show respect to."

Then he looked at me even more intensely as he continued. "And you, Preacher, you ain't jack. As far as I'm concerned, you just like me. The only difference between us is that you wear those expensive suits and I don't. You drive a sweet car, and I don't. You talk your crap from the pulpit, and I talk mess right here in these streets. I wouldn't be surprised if you screwed this pregnant witch. 'Cause you see, preacher man, I ain't got no respect for you. See, all your members don't see you for what you are, but I do. You just another hustling mofo, just like me. So don't think you can ever question me about my grandmama. Because as far as I'm concerned, she is a subject that is null and void with your scandalous self."

I could feel myself getting very angry, but I had to keep in mind what I was here for.

"Well, Cee, that is your opinion, and you have the right to it."

"Yeah, aw-ight. So tell me, where does this ho live?"

"She lives at seventy-one twelve Cherry Street, and she isn't working or doing anything at this time. She lives with her father, but he works a lot of hours. He is hardly ever at home."

I continued to supply him with all the information he needed, and then I gave him a picture of Grace.

"So her old man is hardly ever home, huh? You did your homework, didn't you, Preacher? So when do you want me to do this?"

"As soon as possible. It needs to look like a robbing gone bad so that she will not be able to trace any of this back to my friend. And, remember, I don't want her hurt too badly. Just bad enough for her to lose the baby."

"Aw-ight, I hear ya." He was staring at the picture.

"I mean it, Cee."

"What about the money? I want half now and the other half when I'm done."

Thinking quickly, I told him that I could give him a hundred dollars now and the rest when the job was done. "I can get the rest of the money from him tomorrow night."

Giving him the money, I knew that I had entered into something new for me. He told me that he would take care of everything in the next day or two at the latest.

After our meeting I drove back to my office, quickly locking the door behind me, just in case someone else was in the building. I didn't want anyone to walk in on me.

I walked over to one of the bookshelves and removed a couple of books, revealing the spot where I keep my secret emergency stashes of money. This was an emergency of a new magnitude. After counting out five one-hundred dollar bills, I put the books back in their places.

Unlocking my door and leaving it ajar, I went over and sat at my desk as I went over in my mind today's event.

Chapter 19

When I got home that evening, Teri was just putting the final touches on dinner. She seemed to be floating around the kitchen on a cloud.

"Why in such a good mood?" I asked her.

"Oh, you startled me." She stepped back and grabbed her chest.

"I'm sorry, dear." I walked over to her and kissed her.

"I talked to Mama today, and she is so excited about my visit. She says that she can't wait to see me."

"I've decided to come down at the end of the week and spend the weekend with them," I informed her. "We can spend Sunday with them at church and come back home after that."

"Oh, darling, that's a wonderful idea," she said, beaming.

"I didn't realize this meant so much to you." I gave her a big hug. It was more for my benefit. "Have you decided when you will be leaving yet?"

"Saturday morning, if everything works out," she said, the dinner preparations now complete.

"Sure, Saturday morning is fine. I'll drive you to the airport and see you off. Although I have to admit, it will be oh, so painful to see you leave," I joked halfheartedly.

"Thank you, baby." She took me by the arm. "You will be coming later in the week. Now come and sit down, while the dinner is still good and hot."

"Let me wash up first. I'll be back in a minute." I left the kitchen and headed to the half bath in the hallway to wash up.

After I enjoyed a great dinner of roast beef with potatoes and carrots, I read the newspaper while Teri cleaned the kitchen. Afterward, we retired to the blue room to watch some television. I wasn't very interested in what was on, but she was. It was one of those Lifetime "fall in love and live happily ever after" movies for women. The kind that made me sick.

I just lay back with my wife in my arms, and before long I was asleep. I guess I was snoring too loudly, because after a couple of harsh sighs from Teri, I got the message and moved on into the bedroom.

"There is not much more left of the movie, honey. I'm right behind you," she said, never taking her eyes from the screen.

I decided to take a soak in the spa tub until her movie was over. I was awakened once more by her gently rubbing my neck. Looking up at her, I told her that I didn't realize I was that tired.

"I'm more worn out than I thought I was, I guess."

"Sure you are, darling. You're a very busy man. I think you're working yourself way too hard. Come on to bed, sweetheart." She grabbed a big towel for me to dry off with. She wrapped the towel around me and led me to the bedroom. We just lay there, wrapped in each other's arms, until my right arm lost feeling, in many ways like my heart had.

Chapter 20

As I sat at my desk, I had to admit that it was kind of sad watching Teri's plane take off early this morning. I was really going to miss her these few short days. But at least I could now sit back and wait for Cee to come through for me. I had forced myself to believe that this was something that had to be done.

I was feeling a bit melancholy, lonely, and didn't want to be alone tonight, so maybe I could get in touch with Monica. When I was growing up, it was Mama, my brother, Anthony, and me. Anthony had always had girlfriends and women vying for his attention, for as long as I could remember. We were as different as two brothers could be. I was into the church, and he was into the street life. I was looking forward to going to college, while he could think only about how to get the quick money. I studied hard, while he studied the females. While Mama worked her hands to the bone, he didn't think twice about bringing a beautiful girl home, to our room.

The noises they would make had me suspicious, and even more, I would wonder about what I was missing out on. I guessed in my warped way of thinking, I felt I had to make up for what I had missed out on. I could clearly remember the noises they would make. I was confused, my mind, as well as my body, at times. Those sounds would bring forth all sorts of feelings within me that I never acted on. Yet suppressing them only left me empty. It was such a curious and peculiar time for me. I had to shake off the memories.

After a few seconds I picked up my office phone and dialed her number. Waiting for her to pick up, I scanned my office, thinking, *I really do need to tidy up a bit.* Her answering service picked up. As I was hanging up the receiver, someone stuck her head in my office and said good morning in a happy tone. Looking up, I saw that it was Tyerra Williams. She had come in today and was looking really good this morning, I might add.

"Good morning, Tyerra. How are you this morning?" I sat back in my chair.

"Just fine," she returned with a big smile on her face. "I hope it's all right. Sister Gary told me that I could use the church computer. She has a doctor's appointment, and she won't be in until after eleven o'clock."

"Sure, Tyerra. You should know that you can use the computer anytime. Can I help you with anything?" I asked her, hoping to strike up a longer conversation between the two of us.

"No, thank you," she returned shyly.

"Well, I'll be in my office if you need me."

She stepped out of the office and hurried down to the secretary's office. *Yes . . . if you need anything at all,* I said to myself. I thought she had a little crush on her pastor, anyway. She had come in here, looking all cute and things. I'd just stay close to the office today, just in case she needed something. *Maybe I'll be nice and take her out to lunch,* I thought, checking my calendar. *I do not have any meetings or business to attend to this morning. Great.*

After sitting around the office for an hour, not doing much of anything, I walked down to the secretary's office to find Tyerra hard at work on the computer.

"Excuse me, Sister Tyerra, but I was getting a little hungry, and I was wondering if you would do me the honor of going to lunch with me today."

Looking up at me with the face of an angel, she shyly said, "Pastor, I do have an awful lot of work to do and—"

Interrupting her before she could finish her refusal, I held my hand up and said, "Sister Tyerra, please don't turn me down. Sister Harris is out of town, visiting her parents, and there is nothing that I hate more than eating alone." I could see that I was making her somewhat uncomfortable.

"Oh, when did she leave?"

I knew that she wanted to change the subject.

"She left this morning, at seven. Now, does this mean that I have a lunch guest?"

"I really do need to get this done as soon as possible. . . ."

I could see her mind working to come up with excuses.

"Well, will it make you more comfortable if we order something and we eat right here in the office?" I was hoping that this would put her more at ease.

"Sure." I watched her release her breath. "That will be fine." She finally smiled once again.

"So what would you like to eat? I'll let you choose today," I informed her.

"I don't know. I'm not really in the mood for anything special."

"I'll just be in my office, and you can take care of everything. Just let me know when it gets here. Anything that you choose will be all right with me. I'm not a hard person to get along with." I winked at her and returned to my office.

After about forty minutes she knocked on the door and entered my office. "Pastor, I hope Chinese food is all right. They were close by, and I knew they would be quick. The food at Eastern China is pretty good, also." She was carrying the food awkwardly in the box that it was delivered in.

"Chinese is fine," I assured her.

"I ordered shrimp fried rice and egg rolls, nothing too exotic." She laughed nervously.

"It all sounds and smells good to me. Come on over to the couch, and let's enjoy this good food." I got up from my desk and directed her to the couch. After she placed the food on the coffee table, I blessed it and gave thanks to the Lord for such a lovely lunch mate. I could still feel that she was somewhat ill at ease. So we talked frankly about her classes and her family.

She told me that she and all her siblings were named after their father, Deacon Tyrone. With her being the oldest and a girl, she was named Tyerra. Her brothers' names were Tyrone Jr., Tyrell, Tyresse, and Tyrick. Her two sisters were named Tychelle and Tyrica. She was a twin to Tyrick. Now, why in the world would a parent want to do something like that to their children? I would never figure that one out.

She went on to tell me that she was starting to feel burned out with the full load she was carrying at school. And she said something about being overwhelmed. I wasn't paying that much attention; I was too busy staring into her baby-doll eyes and watching the way the grease from the food made her pouty lips look so sensuous. I wasn't paying much attention to anything that she was saying anymore. If she only knew the power she possessed with those eyes, I thought.

"I'm sure you can handle it, Tyerra," I said, getting ahold of myself. "You are a very smart young lady, and I have full confidence in you." I nodded slightly and gave her a quick wink. "Tyerra, you are also a very pretty young lady."

She stopped nibbling on her egg roll and looked down at the floor.

"I didn't say that to make you feel uncomfortable, sweetheart. I just felt the need to tell you this. There are going to be a lot of young men out there trying to come at you the wrong way, and you have too much to offer. You are pretty, you have positive goals, and you are working very hard in school. From what I can see of you, I can almost guarantee that you can do whatever it is you put your mind to. I see success in your future. You're going to make some young man a wonderful wife. The right young man."

"Thank you." She smiled cautiously. Her shyness was a big part of her appeal. She couldn't look up at me. She continued to look down at what was left of her meal.

"You're welcome," I said, looking into her eyes. *And I do mean every word of it,* I thought. I couldn't help staring at her eyes. I didn't say anything, and she looked up and away a few times, but I knew that she was feeling me.

"Good afternoon, y'all," came a thunderous voice, breaking the hypnotic trance. "What y'all eating in here?" She was breathing like a Brahman bull.

"Oh, good afternoon, Sister Gary. We were just eating some lunch, Chinese food. Some shrimp fried rice and egg rolls. We have a little left if you would like some," I said, madder than a hornet that she had interrupted our lunch. "I had to beg Sister Tyerra here to keep me company." I stood to straighten my pants.

"I had better clean up this mess so that I can get back to my report," Tyerra said, scrambling about nervously.

"I want to thank you again, Sister Williams. You were very nice company. Hopefully, we can finish what we were talking about," I said, smiling in her direction but never taking my eyes off Sister Gary, who was eyeing the leftover food.

"Okay," Tyerra said and hurried past Sister Gary and out of the office.

"Can I help you with anything, Sister?" I asked, still heated.

"Ah, no, Pastor. I'm just on my way to the office. I've got a lot of work to make up today."

"You do that," I snapped, still annoyed. She always seemed to bust her nosy self into my office at the wrong time. I sat at my desk and tried to get back to work. She got on my nerves sometimes, man.

Chapter 21

Last night had to be the longest night for me since I'd been married. Teri had been gone only one day. I had taken my wife's company for granted. She called to let me know that she was enjoying herself with her family, and she also admitted that she missed me terribly. I could hear it in her voice that the trip agreed with her. I didn't want her to feel bad about leaving me, so I told her that I loved her, that I missed her, and that I would see her real soon.

I knew that her parents were glad to have their baby girl home, but for me it was a cold cuts sandwich and a glass of cranberry juice, the remote control, and a big, empty house. How pathetic. I fell asleep while sitting on the chaise lounge in the blue room, and yeah, I did dream about Tyerra's sweet little smile and her baby-doll eyes. And then in came Sister Gary's nosy behind, just like always, busting into my office like a herd of wild buffalo.

When I woke up, I called Monica's number from the kitchen as I searched the cabinets for something appetizing. I was bored and had a taste for something, but I just didn't know what. I came up empty, and her answering service picked up again. What was up with that? This was the second time, two days in a row. I grabbed my keys and cell phone and decided it was off to the first fast-food restaurant I saw.

I pulled into the drive-through of a fast-food restaurant, one that I didn't bother to get the name of. All I wanted to know was if they had sausage and egg biscuits and a hot cup of coffee. They did, and I was satisfied. I decided to call Grace and check in on her.

"Yeah?" a gravelly voice answered.

"Good morning, Grace," I said.

She didn't reply.

"How are you feeling this morning?" I asked, not really caring. I just wanted to give her the false sense that I did.

"I feel horrible. Why?"

Taking a chance, I decided to ask her if there was anything I could do for her. I hadn't spoken to her going on two weeks.

She laughed at my question and asked, "Haven't you done enough?"

"Well, I did tell you that I would call and check on you, remember?" I took a big bite from my breakfast.

"Oh, yeah. Well, don't put yourself out too much for me," she returned.

I could tell that she was in a very foul mood this morning. Her pregnancy must've been getting to her.

"Why are you so mean to me, Grace? I'm trying to help you."

"Oh, you are?" I could tell she was being sarcastic again, and I didn't feel like listening to it.

"I can see that you aren't feeling well. Maybe I should call you back later."

"Whatever, Reverend Harris."

I hung up the phone in her ear. Yeah, she was in rare form this morning. Maybe it was morning sickness, which I had heard pregnant women go through. Or maybe she was just trying to be a pain in my butt. I was starting to get that hollow feeling in my stomach again, and I was starting to rethink this whole Cornell deal. I couldn't let her have this baby and take a chance on losing my wife and my church. I had never slipped up this badly, but this baby would be my baby, my flesh and blood.

I wasn't so hungry anymore, so I tossed what was left of my breakfast into a curbside garbage bin. I had too much on my mind. I decided to go to my office and try to get some work done. Maybe it would end up being a good day. Maybe Tyerra would come in today and we could take up where we'd left off when Sister Gary interrupted things. Checking my watch, I saw that it was 8:38 a.m. and I had wasted enough time already.

Chapter 22

Neither Sister Gary nor Tyerra was in the building this morning. I should have known that that girl would be in class at this hour. After settling down, I was surprised that I was able to get a lot of work done, thanks to no distractions. I had so much on my mind. Right before noon my cell phone rang, and again it was a number that I did not recognize.

"Hello?" I answered hesitantly.

"Yeah, preacher man, your friend ready to pay a nigga?"

It was Cornell. My stomach dropped. "Cee?" I whispered.

"Yeah, it's me. Who did you think it was? I need my money. And let me tell you something. That witch knows how to throw them bones."

I couldn't say a word. I just held the phone up to my ear. I had just spoken to her last evening. My mind was running a mile a minute.

"Are you there, man?" he yelled into my ear.

I couldn't respond.

"I went over to the address that you gave me, thinking that I was going to push this ho around some. And the ho had the nerve to fight me like a man! I'm gonna have to stay on the DL for a few days. I don't want nobody thinking that some raggedy tramp hung with me. So, preacher man, when can I get paid?" He was sounding very impatient, as well as upset.

"I, uh . . . I have your money, Cee. Where are you?"

"I'm at a pay phone right now, but I can tell you where to meet me."

After I jotted down the information on a piece of paper and hung up, I walked over to my hiding place in my office. I took out five one-hundred dollar bills, grabbed my jacket, and rushed out the door, running smack into Sister Gary.

"Sorry, Pastor. I didn't see you," she said, out of breath.

"Yeah, yeah, that's all right," I said, trying to get around her wide hips.

"Are you on your way to a meeting or something?" There she went again, trying to be nosy.

"I have an appointment." I headed to the door.

"Okay. I guess I can handle things around here." She stood in the doorway, looking at me with confusion on her face. It was as if she was trying to read my thoughts.

"I don't mean to be rude, Sister, but I am in a big hurry."

"I understand. You just go on to your appointment," was the last thing that I heard her say before I was in my car and pulling out of the parking lot.

I knew that I didn't have a lot of time to think about this thing, but now that it had happened, there was no turning back. I hadn't thought that poor Grace could possibly get killed dealing with a monster like Corn . . . Cee. He didn't care about anything, he had told me. That boy hated the world and everybody in it. Except for his grandmother. *What have I done, oh, Lord? What in the world have I done to that poor girl?*

Chapter 23

When I drove into the neighborhood that Cee had given me directions to, I was reminded of why I didn't come to this part of the city much. The dilapidated buildings, the people standing around with a look of hopelessness and despair written on their faces . . . No one seemed to have anywhere to go, and most of them were just hanging around on the corner or in front of the crumbling buildings. Some were sitting on the front stoops or hanging out their windows. All of them were waiting for something to happen, something to take place. . . . What? I guessed I would never know.

Pulling up to the address scribbled on the piece of paper, I took a long hard look at the building. I couldn't imagine anyone living in this place. The dismal building looked like it should have been condemned by the city years ago. It might be better if it were burned to the ground. I was having second thoughts about parking my car in front of the place. I wanted to pull away, but I knew that I had to get this business with Cee behind me. Now more than ever.

After sitting in my car for about three minutes, studying the faces of the people, who were also studying me, I opted to honk my horn. After a few seconds Cee came walking out of the front of the building, looking like he had been through hell and back. He had scratches all over his face. His hair was all over the place. Yes, he was in bad need of a haircut. When he got into my car, I couldn't help but stare in awe at the wounds on his face and neck for a few minutes. I quickly thought about my friend Detective Riley and how he had told me time and time again that DNA evidence had busted so many criminals. But this was too much. This was too deep. The slamming the car door broke my reverie and brought me back to the situation in front of me.

"My goodness, man! What in the heck happened to you?"

He was more than a little annoyed. "Man, I told you that that ho could throw down, didn't I?"

I didn't know if I was scared to find out what had happened or if it was just nervousness, but I laughed right in his face as I started the car.

"Where are you going, man?" he asked me.

"You don't expect me to leave my car here, the way these people are looking at me do you?"

"Preacher, calm the heck down. Ain't nobody gonna mess with your car."

"Are you sure?" I asked him with much reservation.

"My boys got this here on lock, ya hear?"

"What?" I asked, without taking my eyes off the crack zombie who was staring at me like I was her next hit.

"I told you that we got this on lockdown. Nobody does a thing unless we say so, and you need to remember that. That's why nobody better ever, and I mean ever, hear about that trick doing this to me. And, by the way, the price of the job just went up, you know. . . . I might need to buy a Band-Aid or something like that. That tramp tried to mess up my pretty face." He was looking over his scratched image in the rearview mirror.

"I'll pay you what we agreed on, Cornell, and that's that."

"It's Cee!" He leaned in closer to me. "You should have told me about that wild ho! I thought she was gonna be some little lightweight. You didn't bother to tell me that she could fight like a man."

"I didn't know anything about that," I told him, turning the car's motor off. I was feeling bad about his situation. I tried to brace myself for what I was about to hear after asking him the next question. "What happened when you went over there?" I sat back, readying myself to listen.

"I went over to the address that you gave me," he began. "I knocked on the door. At first I kinda had second thoughts because the ole girl was kinda fine, you know, even in the morning and in her robe. She looked pretty nice. I told her that my car had broken down and that I needed to use her phone. I could tell that she didn't want to trust me and all." He was still studying his face in the mirror. "She let me in, anyway. I called my boy that had parked up the street. Then I asked her if she could give me something to drink. When she walked into the kitchen, I followed and she gave me a glass of water. I didn't want no water. But I started a conversation with her. I asked her if she was married, and she told me no. I asked her if she lived by herself, and she told me no again.

"She told me that her father was there, getting ready for work, and I got a little scared. But then I could tell that she was lying to me to get me to leave. I asked if it was all right if I waited for my ride at her house, and she told me something about her getting ready to go somewhere. I figured that I didn't have much time, so I asked her if she had any money. She just stood there, staring at me, like she was crazy or slow or something. So I started pushing her back into the living room. That was when her crazy butt started fighting me and stuff. You know, I could have killed that dumb ratchet. . . ."

I was starting to feel sick to my stomach as I listened to his account of what had happened.

"She started scratching me all in my face and swinging like she was crazy. Man, I tell you, I tried to choke the heck out of her. But she just kept coming at me like a mad person. She got up and tried to run, but I grabbed her by her hair and dragged her back into the living room. Then she started screaming, and I panicked. So I started beating her in her face. I dragged her in the bathroom, and she started fighting me again. I was about to say, 'Forget this,' but she made me even madder. All I wanted to do was make her pay. So I tried to beat the snot out of her. I threw her against the sink, and she bent over like she was really hurt. It was her back or side or something.

"But her stupid butt was still trying to come at me. Can you believe that? She was still hanging with me, and I tell you that ain't no ho ever hung with me that tough. Then I said, 'Enough of this.' I took her and threw her into the tub. I mean, I beat the heck out of her. I beat her in her face. I beat her in her stomach. I mean, I tried to beat the life out of her. If there was a baby in her stomach, I doubt if there is one in there now. I didn't realize that I had beaten her so badly, because I was mad. She was bloody as heck, man. Blood was all over that bathroom when I left. But I made sure that she was still breathing. I know for a fact that she was still alive when I left.

"Man, your friend owes me a lot for what I had to go through with his ho. When I looked out and saw my boy up the street, I signaled for him to pick me up. I made sure that no one was out. I don't think anybody saw me. Man, I have been hiding out here ever since. But I know that nobody saw me. They don't know nothing 'bout me in that hood, anyways. Me and my boys don't hang in that part of town. Niggas over there are weak and got the nerve to call themselves the L Block Maniacs. Man, them dudes are weak."

I was so sick I felt like I wanted to throw up while he spoke. "Heck, Cornell! Are you sure you didn't kill her?" I was on the verge of panic. I didn't know what might have transpired since I first heard the news.

"Naw, she was still breathing when I left, but I should have killed her for scratching me up like this. And, nigga, if I have to tell you about my name one more time!"

I couldn't believe his mind-set. He had the nerve to be upset with her. I wanted to go right then and there and find out how Grace was doing.

"Now, where is my money? Tell your friend that this was not an easy job and I'm gonna need about seven or eight hundred dollars for the hell I went through. I mean, a nigga needs to get paid for pain and suffering. I know your boy heard about pain and suffering, ain't he?"

"I have five hundred fifty dollars on me right now." I took it out of my jacket pocket.

He snatched it out of my hand and counted it right in front of me, like he couldn't trust me. He jumped out of the car, but before shutting the door, he turned to tell me that he would be waiting for the rest of his money. "I got your number, preacher man, and I will be calling you. You need to tell the ole boy that I said, 'Thanks for the job,' but the next time he should hire Mike Tyson if he wants to go around screwing a crazy tack head."

He then shoved the money down in his jeans pocket and turned to walk up the steps of the dilapidated building, as if he had no cares in the world.

I drove out of that part of town and headed home. I needed to be alone tonight to think through everything that had taken place. When I reached the house, I didn't even bother turning on any lights. I just walked straight to my bedroom and sat on the side of my bed, holding my head in my hands, wondering how I could have let something like this happen. Wondering how I could let myself get involved with someone like Cornell Hollis.

Chapter 24

I lay around the house for what seemed like hours, until my stomach reminded me that I hadn't eaten for a while. Looking through the refrigerator, I grabbed some green seedless grapes and rinsed them off in the sink. Then I walked into the blue room and turned on the television. Nothing seemed to catch my interest, so I turned it off and continued to eat my grapes.

My mind stayed busy as I thought about what that silly thug Cornell had told me he'd done to Grace. I couldn't stop thinking about that poor girl. What did I do to her? She did not deserve what had happened to her. She didn't deserve to get beaten down like a dog. That darn Cornell was an animal. He acted like an animal, he thought like an animal, and he lived like an animal. But this whole thing was my entire fault. A pang hit me in the gut. I kept thinking about her lying there, covered in blood, her face beaten in like she was a common criminal on the streets. What did her poor father think when he walked into the house after working hard all day to find his only child in such a condition? I threw what was left of the grapes on the table. I guessed I wasn't so hungry, after all.

While I was trying to force myself to think of other things, the phone rang, and sparks of irritation shot through me. I did not feel like talking, but I couldn't just let it ring. I was the pastor, and one of my members could really need me. Brother Dixon might need me. With each ring, it felt as if someone was punching me in the stomach.

I answered, not knowing what to expect on the other end.

"Hi, sweetheart. What are you doing?"

Relieved that it was my wife, I let out a sigh. "Oh, Teri, baby, it's you! I was just sitting here eating some grapes and watching television."

"Grapes? That's not much of a meal." She sounded concerned.

"I know that, baby, but I was just lounging around the house and grabbed something to munch on."

"Okay, sweetie, but grapes? I see now that you do need for me to take care of you, don't you?"

"I sure do, honey," I said, and at that moment I meant it more than anything else in the world. "I wish you were here or that I was there with you. I love you, and I miss you. How's the family?"

"Everything is fine here, but I'm worried about you, is all."

"Please, baby, don't waste any of your time worrying about me. I want you to enjoy yourself. Enjoy the time that you are spending with your family. I'll drive up soon enough."

"I can't wait, darling," she cooed into the phone. "But will you promise me one thing?"

"All right. What is that?"

"Promise me that you will try to eat a little better so that you won't get sick."

I promised her that I would, and she gave me the run-down on all the activities of her day. Boy, did I miss her.

"You have made my evening," I told her.

"And you mine, my love." Then she hung up.

The steady buzz on the line gave me a very lonely feeling. After placing the receiver on the phone's base, I gave the television one more try, but nothing seemed to pique my interest. The phone rang again, and I rushed to answer it, hoping that it was Teri calling back to tell me something that she had forgot to say earlier. It felt like a brick wall was falling in on me when I realized that it wasn't her voice.

"Hello, Pastor. How are you getting along this evening? This is Sister King. I was just calling to see if there was anything I could do for you. I know that Sister Harris is out of town. I can bring you over some dinner or something if you like. Maybe straighten up the parsonage. You know, if you need anything, all you have to do is call. And that's anytime, Pastor," she said in what I was sure she felt was a seductive voice. But years of smoking cigarettes had taken away seduction or anything else that her voice might have once carried.

"No, thank you, Sister. Sister Harris made sure that I would be very comfortable while she is out of town."

"Are you sure, Pastor?"

"Yes, I'm very sure," I said, hoping that she would get the message.

I did have some discretion. Shoot, Sister King was at least ten years older than me, and it showed with every line in her face and the heavy bags under her eyes. I did love a dark chocolate woman, but her skin was like burnt leather. Her husband was at least twenty years older than she was, if not thirty. And he could barely stay awake during service. The poor lady was horny as a rabbit. But I was not the one. She couldn't turn me on if she had a switch. She was not attractive to me at all. As a matter of fact, she reminded me of the mongoose that I saw on the Discovery Channel the other day. That poor mongoose. I doubted that she would be attractive to many of the men in my congregation.

"I am sure," I said, stressing each syllable, before hanging up the phone.

I have got to get out of this house, I thought. *This thing is going to drive me insane if I don't find out something soon.* I went into the bathroom to take a quick shower and find something to get into. Maybe I should stop over at the Good Old Boys Club. I was sure that Deacon Sam and his friends would be there, enjoying themselves, until late. The club was more like an old run-down building, and a few of my friends and I had got together and fixed it up the inside. It was established for us and for our entertainment only. What happened at the club stays at the club. Maybe I would have a few drinks and check out who they had dancing in the VIP room. Yeah, the club always seemed to boost my spirits. So, I sprayed on some cologne and headed to the Good Old Boys Club.

Chapter 25

This morning, when I woke up, I had one of the worst headaches that I'd had in a long time, and I didn't have anything in the house to relieve it. I lay around and did nothing all morning, but my headache didn't seem to want to subside. I decided to get up off my butt and run over to the pharmacy down the street a ways, at the strip mall.

Once there I was in a state of total confusion. They had so many different over-the-counter pain relievers that it was making my headache worse. *This is the reason that I have Teri handle these sorts of things,* I mused. I must have been standing there for about twenty minutes when a young woman walked up to me and asked if I needed her assistance.

"Reverend Harris, I thought that was you. Can I help you with anything?"

Looking up, I peered into the biggest, prettiest smile. "Excuse me?" I said.

"You're Reverend Harris, right?" she asked, extending her right hand.

"Well, yes, I am." I took her hand.

"My name is Sharand Lewis. I have visited your church a couple of times."

"You have? Now, I am sure that I would remember a beautiful smile like yours." I felt corny after making that statement.

"Thank you." She smiled coyly. "I moved to the city a few months ago, and I'm in the process of looking for a church home. I have to admit, I'm leaning toward Unity."

"I certainly hope that you are still considering Unity. We have so much to offer," I told her.

"Yes, and I always feel so comfortable there. You have such a wonderful congregation, and the choir is marvelous. I love nothing more than to listen to some good gospel music."

"Great," I said. "You have my personal invitation and are most welcome at any and all times."

"Thank you." She smiled her most gorgeous smile.

"You have a beautiful smile," I said under my breath. "So how do you like our city?" I was hoping to continue this conversation.

"I've spent most of my time here at the pharmacy, working. I'm the new head pharmacist, and I have to spend quite a bit of time here setting up my new system."

Just listening to her speak, I could tell that she was a professional and a classy lady.

"So where are you from?"

"I'm from Clinton, Iowa, but I worked a year in Minneapolis after graduating from the University of Iowa."

"You have got to be kidding me. There aren't any black people living in Iowa," I said, trying my best to stretch out this conversation.

"Oh, yes, Reverend Harris, you would be very surprised."

"Come on now. You are pulling my leg."

We were both pretty much at ease at this point. My plan was working.

"I was just on my way to lunch when I saw you standing here, looking somewhat confused. So I came over to offer you my assistance." She looked down at her watch.

"I see. Well, when I woke up this morning, I had this horrible headache. I just can't seem to shake it, so I came over here to find something for it. They have so many things out now, I don't know where to start. I usually let my wife handle this sort of thing." I held a couple of boxes of pain relievers in my hand.

"What type of headache do you have?"

"What type?" Now I was really confused.

"Yes. Is it a migraine headache? Or maybe it is more of a sinus headache?"

"I'm sorry, but I'm not following you."

"Okay, then tell me, where does it hurt the most?" She stepped closer to me. The smell of her perfume was all that I could concentrate on.

"Huh? Oh, I, uh . . ."

"Does it hurt in this area?" She placed her hands on my temples. "Or do your eye or nose areas seem to have more pressure? Is it a throbbing pain, a nagging pain, or more like a stabbing pain?"

Her perfume was intoxicating, and it was difficult for me to concentrate on what she was saying. "Well, uh . . . it's more under the eye and across the bridge of my nose," I told her.

"Okay, we're finally getting somewhere." She smiled. *Oh, my goodness. That smile.*

"This seems to be a sinus headache. This will take care of it for you." She picked up a green box from the shelf. "It has five hundred milligrams of acetaminophen and thirty milligrams of pseudoephedrine. This shouldn't make you drowsy," she said, handing me the package with confidence.

"Thank you, Miss Lewis, or is it Mrs.?" I asked at the same time that I checked out her ring finger. *Good*, I thought. *No ring.*

"No, I'm not married." She smiled innocently enough. "I don't even have a boyfriend yet. I'm still trying to get used to this big city at the present time."

"Miss Lewis, then for helping me out today, I insist on taking you out to lunch."

"That's not necessary. I was just doing my job."

"And I'm just doing mine. As a minister, I would love to help you become more comfortable with our beautiful city."

She looked down at her watch once more, and a frown came over her face and her beautiful smile disappeared.

"Is there anything wrong, Miss Lewis?" I asked, concerned.

"I have spent so much time standing here that I have only about twenty minutes left for lunch. Maybe we can do this another time."

"What time do you get off of work this evening?" I wasn't going to let her off that easy.

"I stay pretty late, till around six or so, because of the new system. Plus, I'm training a new girl this week."

"Miss Lewis, you can try to come up with any excuse that you like, but I'm a persistent man. I'll be here at six p.m."

Apparently shocked at my candidness, she could only say, "I'll be here."

"Great! Then I'll see you at six o'clock." Tossing the box into the air and catching it, I turned and strolled down the aisle to the checkout. "I'm going to have that smile on my mind all day," I said out loud to myself. I couldn't wait until six o'clock and a chance to get to know Miss Sharand Lewis better. My headache was gone, and I didn't even have to take those pills. So I threw them in the glove compartment. *Thank you, Miss Lewis.*

Chapter 26

I spent a considerable amount of my day thinking about Miss Sharand. I couldn't think of much else. I was getting lonely with Teri away, but I thought I had found a remedy for that.

Sitting outside the pharmacy, I could see that it was pretty busy inside and that Miss Lewis might be running a little late. I just hoped that she didn't keep me waiting too long. Six fifteen, six twenty, six thirty-five, and finally she came hurrying out of the store. I was a bit irritated. I didn't usually find myself in the position of waiting for a woman. I honked my horn to get her attention, and she ran over to the driver's side of my car, out of breath.

"Reverend Harris, I am so sorry for keeping you waiting. For some reason we became very busy all at once, and I didn't know how to get in touch with you to let you know."

I was now feeling guilty for getting upset with her.

"That's fine, Miss Lewis. We are still on for dinner, aren't we?"

"I don't know. I mean, I had you waiting all this time. I'm sure you have other things that you would rather be doing."

"No, Miss Lewis. You promised me a dinner date, and a dinner date is what I want." I smiled up at her. "After all, you need a good, hot meal after such a long hard day at work," I added.

"I don't know," she began. But before she could come up with any more excuses, I reached over and opened the passenger-side door. "Now, Miss Lewis, please don't keep a hungry man waiting any longer."

She released a deep breath, and I could clearly see that her mind was still at work.

"Come on now," I said.

"All right!" She finally gave in and walked around to the passenger side of the car.

"So what do you feel like eating?" I asked as I turned the key in the ignition.

"I'm not that picky," she answered.

"I know where we can get the best soul food in the city—"

"No thanks," she said, cutting me off. "If you don't mind, I'd rather go for something quick and easy."

"Quick?" I was shocked. "You mean to tell me that I have been looking forward to this all day and you just want to grab something quick?"

"I just don't want you going out of your way for me. Like I told you, I was just doing my job. You are really taking all this way too seriously."

"I know that, Miss Lewis. I am a hungry man whose wife just happens to be out of town, visiting her parents. I will admit that after the day that I have had, I am hungry for intelligent conversation. After all, it is only a dinner," I said, wanting to persuade her.

"I just hate to think that I took up your valuable time, when you could have been doing other, more important things." She was looking out the passenger-door window as the sun was starting to set and the sky was growing dusty in color.

"To me, this is very important, and I feel that you should have a decent meal on me tonight."

She relaxed in her seat and smiled warmly in my direction. "I guess you're right. It's just a dinner." She clicked the buckle of her seat belt.

"Yes, it is a dinner between two friends," I said as I pulled out of the parking lot of the pharmacy.

Seven minutes later I was pulling into the parking lot of the Olive Basket, a small Italian restaurant. "I hope you like Italian food." I glanced at her profile.

"I love Italian food," she told me.

"Great! Then let's go in and find a table. I have been here only a couple of times, but I remember the food being very good."

I rushed to open the door for her and assisted her out of the car. As we walked through the door of the restaurant, I could see right away that this was one of their slow nights. This suited me just fine, since I wanted Miss Lewis all to myself, anyway.

I could smell the heavy aroma of garlic cooking in olive oil, vegetables, and heavy sauces as soon as we were seated. The place was dimly lit, and the owners had tried their best to give it the look of one of those old Italian bistros from the movies. The small tables were covered with red-and-white checkered tablecloths, and an old wine bottle with a melting candle stood atop each. It was small and cozy. On one side of the room was a small wooden bar that had several different bottles of wine hanging overhead. Sharand chose a table by the window so that she could look out during dinner.

A short, plump woman with a face of worn leather came over to our table with two glasses of ice water. "I will give you two a few minutes before I come to take your order," she announced with a light Italian accent when she saw Sharand going over the wine list.

"Thank you," we both said in unison, which made us laugh.

"Umm . . . it really smells good in here," Sharand commented.

"Yes, it does."

"Do you know what you are going to order?" she asked as she looked over the menu. I could see that she was slowly letting her guard down. "Nothing fancy for me," she went on. "Just a salad and lasagna with a glass of wine. Oops! I'm sorry. I will have a Coke with my dinner."

We were both laughing at this point.

"A glass of wine sounds good," I told her. "And I will have the same thing that you are having." I placed the menus to the side. I raised my hand to get the waitress's attention.

After placing our orders, it was time to get to know more about her.

"So, Miss Lewis, tell me about yourself."

The leather-faced woman came back shortly to place a glass of red wine in front of each of us. Sharand took a sip of her wine, and as the wet wine settled on her top lip and her tongue slowly wiped it away, I noticed how delicious her lips looked. *Oh, my goodness,* I thought and had to take a sip of my own wine.

"I feel that I may have helped to persuade you to have wine with your dinner." She smiled. "I hope that your congregation can forgive me," she joked.

"I'm sure they will." I smiled back at her. "I am a man of God, Miss Lewis, but first and foremost, I am a man. Did you know that our loving Savior Jesus himself partook of the grape?" I was trying to keep the conversation upbeat.

"No, I didn't. But I must insist that you call me Sharand, okay?"

"Sure, Sharand. Now tell me about yourself," I said.

"Well, there is not much to tell you." She took another sip of her wine. "I'm really not an interesting person at all. I was born in Des Moines, Iowa. My parents moved to Clinton when I was six. My father was called to pastor the First Baptist Church there. He, my mom, my sister, and two brothers are still there. One of my brothers is studying law at the U of I. My sister is still in high school, but she has already been accepted at Iowa State. She wants to become a dentist. My parents didn't go to college, but they always stressed the importance of having a good solid education."

I watched intently as she talked and sipped her wine.

"Since the day I was born," she went on, "my parents told me that I was going to go to college. I didn't have a choice in the matter."

I watched with anticipation as her tongue glided slowly across her top lip.

"Were you the only African American family in your town?" I asked, wanting to keep her talking.

"Oh, no. As a matter of fact, I am proud to say that Clinton, Iowa, has an African American mayor. And she is a woman."

Almost choking on my wine, I had to take a breath. "There you go again, pulling my leg," I said.

"I wouldn't do that." She shook her head. "Iowa has a rich African American heritage. My grandparents were born in a small coal-mining community called Buxton. It's located about twenty miles south of Des Moines. Buxton was incorporated not long after the emancipation of the slaves. Several newly freed slaves from the states of Maryland and Virginia settled there."

I was really interested in what she was saying, but I couldn't take my eyes away from her mouth.

"Buxton was eighty- to ninety-five percent black, depending on who's telling the story. Most of the men worked in the coal mines. The children went to school, and Buxton even had an African American sheriff. As a matter of fact, my great-grandfather and a couple of his brothers played for the Buxton Wonders, a Negro League baseball team that traveled and played other teams in the league. Such notables as Madam C. J. Walker and

Mr. Booker T. Washington visited the first incorporated YMCA in the state there."

"I would have gone the rest of my life believing that Iowa was one of the last of the all-white states," I told her, my head feeling light from the wine.

"Oh no," she stated proudly. "Iowa has a wonderful African American history."

"Why did you decide to become a pharmacist?" I asked her as the waitress placed our meals in front of us.

"Well, I thought that I wanted to become a doctor, but after going through my grandmother's lengthy illness and ultimate death, I realized how it affected the people around her. Even the doctors were moved. She was one sweet lady." She paused to look out the window. "I felt that if I became a doctor, I would be responsible for the lives of people. Sorry, but that's too much pressure. Don't get me wrong. My hat goes off to all the good doctors out there, but I don't think it's for me."

"I understand," I told her. "But you do know that it is God who holds the power of life and death?"

"I realize that, but people do put a lot of faith in their doctors."

Wanting to change the subject, I asked her how she liked living in the city so far.

"It's going to take me a while to get used to it, I hate to admit. When I came here, I came alone, without any family or friends. I have made a couple of friends at work, but it's not quite home yet. And I hate to admit another thing." She smirked. "I still get lost a lot."

"I find that's the best way to learn the city." I laughed.

Before we realized it, we had talked for so long that we had finished our dinner and were the only customers left in the restaurant.

"I better pay the bill and get you home," I said as I scanned the room.

After we paid the bill and left a sizable tip, the leather-faced woman finally smiled and asked how we liked our meal.

"Delicious, as always," I told her.

"The food here is great," Sharand added.

"We hope you will come back soon, and, may I add, the two of you make a very handsome couple," she said before turning to clean our table.

Looking at each other, we both figured that it would be much easier just to say thanks and leave.

"So, Sharand, what are your plans for tomorrow?" I asked, taking a chance. I could tell that my question caught her off guard. "I'm asking because I find your company interesting and I would love to spend more time with you to get to learn more about you. I would love to hear more about Iowa."

"Reverend Harris, this is so unnecessary. Maybe it's not such a good idea."

"And why not?" I was trying to think fast, despite the wine working on my head.

"For one thing, I feel like I may be taking advantage of your kindness."

"Look, I would have probably eaten a cold cuts sandwich in front of my television if you hadn't had dinner with me tonight. Instead, I had a wonderful meal and wonderful conversation. So, you see, you are doing me a huge favor. My wife is going to be away for a couple more days, and all I'm asking for is dinner between friends."

"I don't know about this."

"Sharand, look, I promise I won't bite you," I said, crossing my heart with my finger.

"I'll see," she said softly. I wasn't going to take no for an answer.

"I'll pick you up at six, or will six thirty work out better?"

After several seconds of silence, she finally said, "Six will be fine."

I pulled into the pharmacy parking lot, and she pointed to where she had parked her silver Toyota Camry. I told her that I hoped I wasn't making her feel uncomfortable. I could see that she was.

"I know special people, and you are very special. I just want to be your friend. We can all use friends." I gave her my best boyish grin.

She tried to smile. "You're right," she said as she opened the car door.

"And, Sharand . . ." She turned to face me. "Thank you once more for a wonderful evening."

"Thank you, Reverend Harris," she said as she stepped out of the Cadillac.

I sat there until she found her key, unlocked her door, and started her car. *I see that she likes silver also,* I thought. She waved to let me know that all was well. I drove home that evening, and I didn't give one thought to Grace, Cornell, or the other problems that were plaguing my life.

Checking my cell phone, which had been turned off all evening, I saw that I had two missed calls. Both were from a pay phone, and I concluded that the calls were from Cornell. I listened to both messages, and both were littered with foul language. *My goodness, he has such a dirty mouth,* I thought. I could see that this young man was trying to wreak havoc on my nerves. *Snap. Forget about him.* All I wanted to think about tonight was Sharand Lewis.

Chapter 27

I woke up feeling great this morning. I called my wife to let her know that I would leave early tomorrow morning so that I could reach Chicago before dark. She told me that she could not wait to see me.

"Same here, sweetheart," I told her.

I had made the decision last night that I wouldn't spend any time over at the church today, since my associate ministers would take care of Sunday's services. All I needed to do was grab some notes from my desk, and I would be out of there.

Sister Gary was in rare form, as usual, this morning, complaining about one thing or another. I wished she would get out of my office and go back to hers so that she could get some work done. I swear, I thought that she was trying to bring my headache back.

As far as I could make out, she was not happy at all with something that Tyerra had done, but that was her problem, not mine. She was the one who had recommended to the deacon board that Tyerra work with her in the first place. My mind would concentrate on only one thing and that was how I was going to get little Miss Sharand Lewis in my grasp.

Sister Gary's voice pierced my thoughts. "Pastor, Brother Dixon has been trying to reach you all morning. It seems somebody broke into his house and beat his poor daughter half to death. I can't believe that somebody beat poor sister Grace like that," she mumbled. "He's been calling for you since yesterday, and he's called a couple of times this morning," she ranted.

"What?" I was quickly brought back to reality.

"Poor Sister Grace is over at Mercy Hospital, sir, and she has been beaten up pretty badly." She kept repeating the word *beaten,* and it seemed to hit me with a powerful punch every time it came out of her mouth.

"Oh, no!" My heart was pounding hard against my chest. I had forgotten all about Grace this morning. It was all my fault. Cornell had beaten her up at my request. "Did he say how she was doing?" I asked hesitantly. It felt like my stomach wanted to cave in.

"She wasn't doing too well yesterday," she answered.

I had to lean over slightly and hold my stomach.

"She has been in a semi-coma but was talking—or at least trying to—last night, they say. Brother Dixon was pretty upset over this whole thing. I couldn't get much out of him. You know how quiet that man is. Trying to talk to him is like trying to talk—"

"What else did he say?" I was on the verge of panic from the guilt.

"Nothing. He has been over there since they brought her in. You know that Brother Dixon doesn't talk much." She never skipped a beat. "I have tried to hold conversations with him since his wife passed, and getting him to talk is like pulling teeth."

She was talking too much and getting comfortable with this conversation. I didn't feel like listening to her babble this morning.

"Do you know a few Sundays ago I asked him—"

That was the last thing that I heard her say. I was up and out the door before she could finish her sentence.

I reached Mercy Hospital and was directed to the IC unit. My heart sank to an all-time low when I saw poor

Brother Dixon trying to get down a cup of coffee in the waiting area. Immediately, I walked over to him and took his hand.

"Brother Dixon, how is she?" I asked, trying to maintain a sense of calm in my demeanor.

Looking tired and frail, he barely shook my hand. "She is trying to hang in there. She was slipping in and out of consciousness all night. The doctors say that she has a good chance of pulling through this because she was fighting all night. They have been monitoring her pretty steadily, and they think she may have damaged her spinal cord, and . . ."

Before he could get another word out, Brother Dixon broke down right there in front of my eyes. I tried to console him as best I could by rubbing his shoulders. I didn't know what to say. I felt as if someone had literally kicked me right in my temples.

"Pastor, the doctors told me that my Grace is pregnant . . . pregnant," he said, repeating the word as if he was trying to convince himself.

My temples were throbbing at a ferocious pace.

"She didn't tell me anything about being pregnant. The doctors don't know if they're going to be able to save the baby. I may have just lost a grandbaby, and I may lose my baby all in the same day." He cried silently as he placed his hands over his face. "This is all my fault," he said, trying to compose himself. "Ever since my wife died, all I've done is work, and I've neglected my daughter. I know she is old enough to take care of herself and all, but she is still my baby."

"No, this is not your fault at all," I told him. "The devil is busy, and we must be prepared for him when he raises his evil head. Do you think they will allow me in to see her?"

"Yes, Pastor. Just follow me." He tried to smooth his clothes nervously. "I let them know that you're our pastor. But I'm sure it won't be a problem." Poor Brother Dixon was so on edge that he didn't know what to do with himself.

After we were given the okay, we entered Grace's room. I approached the bed. *That piece of garbage. Cornell did not have to beat her like this,* I thought as I stood over her. I almost said these words out loud and had to bite my tongue. "My goodness," I finally said. "What kind of animal would do such a thing?"

There was a tube going into her nose and down into her lung. She had a tube in her mouth, and one went into the right side of her neck. Her face was swollen almost beyond recognition, and her eyes were black and purple. Her lips were severely cut. She had an IV in her left arm and air cuffs on both legs. She was in critical condition. This wasn't Brother Dixon's fault. This wasn't his fault at all. This was entirely my fault. It was my fault that this poor girl had gotten pregnant. And it was my fault that she was lying here in this hospital, fighting to hang on to her precious life.

Brother Dixon had once more become overwhelmed with grief and had to walk out of the room. Noticing that I was alone, with only the sounds of the beeping equipment breaking the silence, I decided I had to get through to her to let her know that she had to pull through this. That she was going to come out just fine. Looking down at her hand, I couldn't help but stare at the IV in her arm. There was a monitor on the forefinger of her right hand, so I just touched her right arm.

"Grace, can you hear me?" My voice cracked. "Grace, honey, I am so sorry for all of this. I just know in my heart that you are going to pull through this. Because if you don't, I don't know what I am going to do." I thought

I saw a tear run down the side of her face. I should have thought this through thoroughly before I called Cornell and pulled him into this, I said silently to myself. *I am going to have to deal with this b—.*

I felt so guilty that I needed to pray. I went into the waiting area and brought Brother Dixon back into the room. I took him by the hand to let him know that I wanted to pray. "Dear Heavenly Father," I began to pray. I didn't know if I was praying more for her or for myself. "Please, Father, strengthen this poor child's father so that he may get through this also," I continued. I prayed and I prayed. I prayed for forgiveness. I prayed for a healing of broken hearts, minds, bodies, and souls.

After I finished, I felt drained. Brother Dixon and I went back out to the waiting area, and he fell asleep sitting up in a chair. I needed to find Cornell Hollis. I barely touched Brother Dixon's shoulder, and he mumbled a few words and woke up.

"Brother, there is really nothing else that we can do right now. Why don't you go on home and get yourself some rest?" I told him.

"I can't leave until I know that my baby is going to be all right," he said with an abundance of sadness in his eyes. "I can't leave until then, Pastor."

Knowing that I wasn't going to change his mind, I opted to leave it alone. He thanked me for coming and for my words of prayer. I told him that I was his pastor and reassured him that all would work out.

"Can I offer to buy you a hot meal from the cafeteria?" I asked him.

"No, thank you," he returned. "I couldn't eat a thing right now. I'm afraid that my stomach may not be able to hold it down."

"I see. Well, I'm going out of town tomorrow to pick up Sister Harris, but if you need me, I can change my plans."

"Don't change your plans on account of us. Your prayers are what we need the most."

"It wouldn't be a problem, no problem at all." I patted him on the shoulder for reassurance.

"I want you to go and be with Sister Harris. We will be just fine," he said, but the words lacked conviction.

"Are you sure?" I said.

"Yes, I'm sure," he said.

I tried to look him in the eye while we talked, but the guilt was eating away at me.

"Okay, but I'll stop by in the morning, before I hit the highway."

"Thank you, Pastor," he said with great sadness in his voice. The guilt was tearing my butt apart by this time, and I had to get out of there. I had to go and find Cornell.

"You take care. Promise me that you will get yourself some rest. Grace is a strong girl, and she is going to pull through this just fine. She is going to need for you to be strong and healthy also." I still had my hand on his shoulder.

"Yes," he said in a whisper.

"I will see you in the morning, all right?"

He could only nod his head. I knelt on one knee right there next to him, and I prayed for strength, wanting the Lord to cover him with His strong arms of protection.

As soon as I was finished, I had to take out a handkerchief to wipe my own face. But before I knew it, I was on the elevator and out the lobby. I was on a mission to find Mr. Cornell Hollis.

Chapter 28

Tearing out of the hospital parking lot, all I could do was think about what I was going to do and say to Cornell when I saw him. Why would he leave that girl in such a mess? I'd told him just to push her down or something. I headed to the run-down neighborhood where I'd met up with him the other day. I didn't have any other way of getting in touch with him. He always contacted me from a pay phone. I parked near the deteriorated building he had come out of the last time we talked.

I was so upset that I didn't worry much about the people hanging around this morning. I just wanted to catch up with Cornell so he could explain to me why he had left her for dead. After sitting in my car for what seemed like hours, I finally saw Cornell swaggering up the block, drinking a tall can of beer from a brown paper bag. Just looking at him made my blood boil. I couldn't believe it. He had on the same clothes from yesterday. He had a pocket full of money, and he had on the same clothes. And he was looking pretty rough, I might add.

He had to be mighty high, because he hadn't even noticed my car. I was sure he had been keeping himself pretty high with the money. As he got closer, I tapped the horn. He looked over in my direction, and once he noticed that it was me, he picked up speed. Snatching the passenger door open, he plopped down in the seat. A horrible odor assaulted my nostrils. He smelled like a week's worth of funk. I had to let my window down.

"I see that you haven't been taking care of yourself," I told him. All he did was laugh and rub his face. "I just came from the hospital where I saw Grace Dixon this morning. You beat her up pretty badly, didn't you?"

"Ain't that what your friend paid me to do?" His words were slurred.

"You left her in bad shape, man."

"I sure did, and you haven't paid me all my money, either." Spit flew from his mouth onto my front window.

"I just wanted you to push her around. She was supposed to lose her baby, not her life."

Looking at me with a surprised expression on his face, he sat up straight. "That witch was alive when I left her house! She didn't die, did she?" He started fidgeting. "Come on, man. I ain't taking no murder case."

We sat quietly as a police car slowly rode by, the officers staring into my car at us.

"I ain't going back to prison for nobody," he continued after the car drove by.

He was getting so jumpy that he was making me nervous. I calmly told him that she was not dead—at least, not yet—that she was barely hanging in there.

We sat quietly for several minutes, both trying to come to terms with what we had done.

"I need to know . . . what happened," I said, breaking the silence.

"What you mean? I told you the broad zoned out on me. She was fighting me like she was a man. You see how she got my face all jacked up. I had to tell my boys that it was my mom on one of her drug binges and that I didn't want to hurt her."

"They are trying to save her baby. She hasn't lost it yet, but they are sure that she will," I told him.

He chose to ignore the statement. "When am I gonna get the rest of my money, Preacher?" he asked, spit hitting me in the face.

"You didn't do a good job, Cornell."

"I told your dumb butt to call me Cee, nigga—"

"You were paid more than what we agreed on," I said, cutting him off. "And you did a sloppy job."

"Look, man, don't BS me. Preacher, you still owe me some more money."

He was all up in my face by this time. My emotions bordered on anger, anxiety, and fear.

"Heck, I did what you told me to do, so you or your friend better come up with the rest of my money or else," he said, threatening me.

"Or else what, Cornell? Are you going to tell on me? Are you going to run to the police and tell them that you beat that poor girl half to death? Yes, you did the job, but you messed it up also." My voice was rising out of control at this point. "You don't deserve any more money."

"Oh, so you gonna play me like that, huh, Preacher?" He was very upset as he stared in my face. "You know what I think? I think that that witch was pregnant with your shorty. Yeah." He nodded. "That's what's up. I told you that I had heard all about your scandalous self while I was on lockdown. Trey was right about you. You are one dirty son of a witch." His whole body shook as he tried to get his words out.

I tried to make him just as angry as he had gotten me. I could see that it was working. "What's the matter, Corn . . . Oh, excuse me. I mean Cee. In the past, whenever I ran into you, you were all dressed up in your name-brand clothes. It was like you were a label whore or something." I laughed in his face. "You seem to be losing it, buddy."

Cornell did not see anything funny about what I had said. He stared at me with eyes that could kill. "Yeah? Well, don't let that bother you, Preacher. I'll be back out there again. Just as soon as these scratches heal on my face. So you don't need to let this bother you at all." His tone sounded low and menacing.

"Oh, it doesn't." The faux smile was still on my face.

"But you do need to worry about your own butt."

His words wiped the smile from my lips. "I am not going to give you another dime. And we better pray that she pulls through this."

"No, you do the praying."

"We better pray that she pulls through this and that she doesn't die," I repeated, although I could tell he wasn't listening to me anymore.

"So it was *your* baby, wasn't it? Man, I swear, you ain't crap." He laughed. "You got my grandmother and other people giving you money. Looking up to your sorry self like you some kinda holy, all-believing Messiah. They be believing that mess you be preaching about from your pulpit. If only they knew you ain't nothing."

I hated to admit that he was touching a nerve or two.

He laughed even harder. Then he shook his head like he was trying to shake off something. "You want to know something?" he went on. "I have to give you your props. You just running game like everybody else, except you got the best game of all." He laughed even harder still. He was starting to scare me. "A pimp and a gangster ain't got nothing on your game! You are one crooked son of a witch, and I ain't gonna sweat you."

Then he turned serious and looked me straight in my eyes. "You will get yours, mutha. Believe that. It's like my grandmother used to tell my mother when she be trippin'. I'm the one holding the leash, and you're the dog. So don't say nothing until I yank your chain. Then that's when I want you to bark, nigga." He stared at me for a few seconds before looking around at the neighborhood.

After getting out of my car, he slammed the door as hard as he could. He ran up the crooked steps of the run-down building, stopping only to drink down what was left in the can he was carrying. Tossing it to the ground, he stretched. Then, not looking back at me even once, he entered the building.

Chapter 29

On the way home, I checked my watch and saw that it was after five o'clock. I had forgotten all about Sharand. I didn't have time to go home to shower and change, and I had practically begged her to have dinner with me again tonight. I'd just tell her that I had had a rough day, and she would understand, I was sure. I felt certain that this evening would go well.

Driving into the pharmacy parking lot, I saw her silver Camry in the same spot as yesterday, so I pulled in and parked next to it. Checking my watch once more, I saw that I had only a few minutes to pull myself together. While waiting, I laid my head back on the headrest, closed my eyes, and tried to relax. I closed my eyes for only a few minutes, or at least that was what I thought. I awoke to her tapping on the window of the car door. Opening my eyes, I looked up right into her gorgeous smile. I was embarrassed but glad to see her. I apologized over and over for letting her catch me asleep the way she had.

"Reverend Harris, you're tired." I sensed she was still trying to get out of the date.

"I could definitely use your company this evening," I told her. "Please get in." I stretched and popped a mint into my mouth. I waited until she walked around the car and got in the passenger's seat. When she was seated comfortably, I asked her if she had any idea of what she wanted to eat tonight.

"Not really." She sighed. "I had a crazy day today."

"Not you too," I said, exasperated.

"Yes, me too." She laughed, making fun of my poor use of the English language. "First, I had to fill out a police report, because some nut thought that he was going to be able to pass a phony prescription. And then someone tried to give us a hard time because they wanted to buy several boxes of cold medicines when they know better. So we had to call the police again. I couldn't believe it, but the creep tried to fight the security guard and tear up the store before the police arrived. They had to Mace him. And then some lady tried to blame me for everything from the Medicare crisis to the war in Iraq! Today was just one of those days. I felt like packing it all up and going back home." She took a deep breath.

This quickly caught my attention. "You can't give up that easily. We all have our good days, and we have our bad days. You're in a job where you are making people's lives better. Believe me, I know better than anyone that people are going to try your nerves every now and again."

"True."

"So let's try to concentrate on the good things that we do for people and that alone, because if we didn't, we would drive ourselves nutty. We have to let the bad stuff just roll off."

"You are right again," she said, laughing and looking out her window. "I'm sorry to hog the conversation with my problems. You said that you had a trying day also."

"I like listening," I assured her, when what I really wanted was for her never to think about leaving again. "Now, have you decided where we are going to eat tonight, since I chose last night?"

"So, you are really hungry, huh?" She was looking at me now.

"Yes, and I have been waiting all day to eat."

"I guess I'm going to have to get used to this big city hospitality." She smiled.

"That's what I like to see. Your smile is so warm and welcoming."

"I'm not all that hungry, and you are. I can afford to lose a few pounds, but your body is great. Oh, my goodness!" She covered her mouth with her hand. "I didn't mean to say that. I'm so embarrassed!" She burst into nervous laughter. "I tend to babble on like that sometimes."

"No need to be embarrassed. I take that as a compliment." I laughed with her.

"Reverend Harris, I have an idea. I have a pot of frozen leftover jambalaya from my visit home last weekend, and you can help me eat it up. I hope that I'm not out of line, but you will have to follow me to my condo."

Jackpot! Bells went off in my head.

"It's not too far from here. It's over by the lake. That is, if you don't mind."

"That sounds great. I love jambalaya."

"Oh, good. You can just follow me."

She jumped out of my car and into hers. As I followed her out of the parking lot, I was as happy as a kid at Christmas. It didn't take long at all before we were pulling up outside her huge condo. It could not get any better than this.

Chapter 30

As I drove into her complex, I could tell right away that this woman liked the finer things in life. I wasn't too familiar with this area. The homes were huge and expensive; the lawns, beautifully adorned with flowers and neatly manicured. Hopefully, I would be spending a lot of time here.

She didn't park in her garage. I assumed that she wanted to walk me through the front door. When I saw her exit her vehicle, I exited mine.

Her condo was gorgeous. The light brick building with blue trim had an immaculately trimmed lawn, and hostas lined the walkway all the way up to her front door. The entire area was very nice.

"This is a pretty large place for just one person," I commented as I approached her.

"Yes, it is, but when I moved to the city, I was pressed. I had to find something rather quickly. I love the fact that it was built in the style of a colonial and that it has so many windows, plenty of windows." She unlocked her front door and let me in.

"You have a beautiful home," I said, looking around. Her entry was clean, bright, and airy.

She led me down the hallway into her spacious kitchen.

"It should only take a few minutes to get everything prepared," she said, hanging her keys on the appropriate peg on a memo board that she had on the wall. "We can either eat in here or go into the dining room. Since I don't have a television in there, I eat most of my meals in here."

"It doesn't matter. Whichever is most comfortable for you."

She paused for a moment. "Since I have company this evening, it may be a good time to break in my new dining room furniture."

"Breaking in" is exactly what I have on my mind, I thought as I smiled to myself. "The dining room will be just fine, then," I said, finally speaking up.

"Make yourself comfortable."

I took a seat at her kitchen island.

She made herself busy by warming the food. "I never asked you what you wanted to go with it." She continued searching her cabinets for dinnerware. She removed a couple of glasses and placed them in front of me. "I can throw together a salad."

I told her that she didn't have to bother with making a salad, that the jambalaya would be enough.

"What about a pot of coffee? Or I have bottled water, grapefruit juice, or cranberry juice."

"You're a woman after my own heart. My favorite drink is cranberry juice."

"Good. Then we will both have cranberry juice. I do have wine, but I wasn't about to offer you any tonight." She beamed as she removed a half gallon bottle of juice from her stainless steel fridge.

"And why not?" I asked.

"Yesterday at the restaurant what you ordered was between you and the Lord. I was not going to be a contributing factor at this meal," she joked.

Laughing along with her, I complimented her on her kitchen. "Everything is so white and sanitary," I said, trying to keep the humor going. I loved the way she had accented it with shades of blue and black.

"Well, I don't have much of a social life these days, and that affords me plenty of time to clean."

"We are going to have to find a remedy for that." I had taken a stab, and I could see her body stiffen at my words.

"Excuse me?"

"I'm just saying that this is a big city, with so many things to do. You're going to have to find something to occupy your time other than your job. You're a beautiful and smart woman. I can't believe that you don't have a long line of men beating a path to your door."

"Thank you for saying that." She removed plates from the cupboard. "But I don't think that is ever going to happen."

"Tell me something. . . . What's wrong with the men in Iowa? Do you mean to tell me that as pretty as you are, not one of them tried to steal your heart?"

She wouldn't respond.

"Come on. Tell me," I said, prodding.

Still, she refused to answer my question. "The food is warm enough now. I just need to grab a few things."

I stood and walked up behind her. "I'm going to ask you one more time," I whispered to the back of her ear. I could feel her body stiffen as I placed my hand on her shoulder. "Have I said anything to offend you, Sharand?"

"No, no. It's just that I'm still trying to move on from my last relationship."

I took the bowl of steaming hot jambalaya from her and grabbed the bottle of juice from the counter.

"Which way to the dining room?" I asked.

She pointed in the direction of the dining room.

"You can get the place settings and glasses," I told her before heading down the hall.

I placed the food and drink on the table and took a seat to study her as she brought in the place settings and ice-filled glasses and arranged them on the table. I could see that I had pretty much struck a nerve, so I waited until she had finished and had taken her seat across from me before I continued the conversation. I wanted to know all there was to know about this gorgeous woman, and I wasn't about to let up now that I had the chance.

"So, Sharand, are you going to talk to me about it? Maybe I can help you in some way."

Pouring the juice in the glasses, she said only that I should bless the food so that we could eat.

"Okay, you win. Let's bless the food."

After I thanked God for a wonderful meal, and my wonderful company for the evening, we started in on the meal.

"This is fantastic," I found myself saying between mouthfuls. "Did you make this?"

"No. Actually, my mom made this, but I have been told that mine is almost as good." She was still somewhat distant.

"You are going to have to let her know from me that she is a culinary genius."

Finally smiling, she responded, "You've only had her jambalaya. It was her dream to become a chef."

"I can tell she knows her way around the kitchen." I scooped another forkful into my mouth.

"She taught me a few things," she stated proudly.

"I am going to have to try your cooking soon, then," I said.

No response.

Placing my fork down and taking a sip of my juice, I sat back in my chair and took a deep breath, holding it for several seconds before releasing it. "Sharand, please forgive me if I have touched a sensitive nerve tonight. I thought that we were friends, and friends can talk about almost anything. I apologize that I think that men have not been beating your door down. You are a very attractive and desirable woman. Forgive me for being truthful."

"Reverend Harris, it's not that. It's just that my ex-fiancé, Jason, and I were supposed to be married when I graduated from school. We were both supposed to move here together. But as you can see, things did not go as planned." She sighed and blew out a breath. I could see the emotions on her face. She was still in pain. "Plus, we didn't have a friendly breakup. I don't like to talk about it much, because even though I hate to admit it, it still hurts quite a bit. I guess that's the reason I work so much." Her face appeared so sad. "I loved him so much, and I gave so much of myself to the relationship. He was my everything."

"That's where you made your mistake," I told her. "God is supposed to be your everything. Not man, woman, or any material things. Could this be the reason that things did not work out between the both of you? You know that our God is a jealous God."

"Maybe," she answered. "I haven't given it much thought."

"Is he the reason you left Iowa?"

"No. I was offered the job as a pharmacist with the corporation right out of college. I had my choice of almost any city, and I pretty much knew that I wasn't going to live in Iowa all my life. I checked out several locations, and this city was the most appealing to me. We were supposed to come here together, but when he decided that we should break it off, take things slower, I came alone. I figured I could make a fresh, new start." She never looked up from her plate.

"I'm glad that you chose to come here. So what is this Jason doing now?"

"I don't know. The last I heard, he had moved to Atlanta and was working as an engineer or something like that. He hated Minnesota. That's where he did his internship. It was too cold up there for him. I didn't mind, as we were still living close enough to our families. So since he didn't stay, I didn't want to move there, either. We had it all planned out." She shook her head. "I'm sure Georgia is warm enough for him. I wish him well in life and all the happiness he can stand. I realize that bitterness only hurts the one holding on to it. But I am homesick." She shook her head.

"You'll be happy again. I'm sure of it." I smiled at her as she quickly glanced up. We had both pretty much had our fill of the meal. "We had better clear this table." I stood, picking up my plate.

"I'll clean this up later." She waved for me to sit back down.

Instead, I walked over to her side of the table. Her eyes were still very sad, but they met mine for a brief second. Without saying a word, I reached for her hand. Before I knew it, we were in each other's arms. My lips were searching for hers as I placed soft, gentle kisses on her face and neck. Every time that I got close to her mouth, she would turn away from me.

"What's wrong?" I whispered.

She tore herself away from my embrace.

"What is it, Sharand?" I was pleading with her to tell me something. "Don't do this. Please talk to me."

I followed her into her living room, where she took a seat in her rose-colored wingback chair. I walked over to her but didn't say anything for several minutes. She placed her hands over her face.

"Are you going to talk to me?" I asked, finally breaking the silence.

"Reverend Harris, this is wrong."

Not wanting to jeopardize my intentions, I walked over and took a seat on her sofa. "I know how you feel, Sharand, and my caring about you is not wrong."

"How can you say that?" Her voice rose, and she was on the verge of crying. "You're a minister and a married man. I'm not going to allow my loneliness to lower my morals. I almost let down my guard with you, and because of that, I would have compromised my beliefs." Looking in my direction but not at me, she said, "Reverend Harris, I think that you should leave now."

Standing, she walked toward her front door. I stood, searching my thoughts, trying to find the right words to convey to her how I felt about her. I reached for her, tried to touch her, but she backed out of the way.

"Don't do this, Sharand. Please."

"Please leave now," was all she said.

I grabbed her hand and moved closer to her. "Is this what you really want me to do?" Once again I tried to find her lips with mine.

"Yes, I do. Please leave now," she answered turning her head away from me.

I sighed heavily. "I have to leave town tomorrow for a few days. Is it all right if I call you in a couple of days?" I asked, never releasing her hand.

"I don't think that would be a good idea."

"I'm not going to stop seeing you, Sharand Lewis. I care a lot about you, and we need to talk about this. I will call you when I get back from Chicago. If you won't give me your number now, then I will drop by the pharmacy every day until you do decide to give it to me."

"You wouldn't do that." With a look of horror on her face, she finally looked up into my eyes.

"Yes, I would—and I will."

"But we've only had two dinners. Reverend Harris, you can't do this."

"You know perfectly well what I mean. I will leave for now, but I will see you when I get back. I am a man who usually gets what he wants. I rarely take no for an answer."

She could only look down at the floor. I left her condo, trying to figure out what went wrong. No woman had ever had the nerve to reject me. But there was a first time for everything. I guessed that I was going to have to work a little harder for this one.

Chapter 31

I stopped in at Mercy Hospital before I hit the highway at 6:00 a.m. I found Brother Dixon asleep again in the same chair that I had left him in yesterday. Not wanting to startle him, I gently touched him on the shoulder. He awoke, groggy and disoriented. I could see that this man was badly in need of some rest.

"Brother Dixon, it is me," I told him. "How is Grace doing this morning?"

Rubbing his eyes and trying to smooth his wrinkled clothes, he informed me that she was doing about the same. "The doctors say that she is a fighter, and she is fighting hard to hang in there."

That's what I want to hear, I thought. "How are you doing?"

"I'm hanging in there. Although I must say that these chairs are not the most comfortable. My back is killing me."

"Can I buy you some breakfast?" I offered.

"I'm not sure if I can eat anything yet."

"Come on. Let us go to the cafeteria. I promise that you'll feel much better if you get something in your stomach."

I could hear his poor old bones crack as he fought to stand up. We both walked down to the hospital cafeteria. I bought sausage, pancakes, and scrambled eggs for both of us. Brother Dixon tried to get down as much as he could, and I was satisfied with the results.

"You were right, Pastor Harris. I do feel a little better," he said, sitting back in his chair, drinking down the last of his hot coffee.

"See, I told you that you would." I felt somewhat better myself. I thought it best to let him sit and think awhile before I said anything more. He seemed to have so much on his mind.

After a few minutes he said, "I have given it a lot of thought, and I think that I could have prevented this whole thing from happening." He had a distant look in his eyes.

My stomach tightened as I waited for what he was about to say.

"Maybe if I hadn't tried to work away my grief and had paid more attention to my home, I could have prevented this."

I thought carefully before I commented. I wanted to say something that would take some of his feelings of guilt away. "Brother Dixon, you know that the Lord will not put more on us than we can bear. He works in mysterious ways. We may never find out why this happened, but He has a plan and we must let His will be done. Every day we are faced with challenges. I have always felt that the Lord is more interested in the way that we react to the challenges. This is how He determines who is strong and who isn't.

"I know that Sister Grace is going to make it through this ordeal. And she is going to be a much better person because of it. She will be a much stronger woman too. You can also draw strength from this, but please, whatever you do, do not blame yourself. When Sister Grace comes home from the hospital, she is going to need you. Now with that said, if you feel that you were not there for her before, make sure that you will be available for her now."

Looking at him, I didn't think he was really listening to a word I was saying.

"I do feel better," he finally said, nodding in agreement. "I don't know if it was the food or not, but I do know for sure that your words have made me feel much better. I feel that the Lord is going to see us through this." He looked up at me. I could see the spark in his eyes.

"He is definitely going to do that," I agreed.

We got to praising the Lord right there in the cafeteria. I almost forgot the reason that the poor girl was there to begin with.

After we went back upstairs and I offered a prayer of thanksgiving, I told him that I had to get on the highway if I wanted to beat the heavy traffic and that I was not a night driver. He assured me that he was going to go home and get some rest, but he was going to wait until his daughter opened her eyes and responded to him.

Knowing that he wasn't going to be persuaded to do otherwise, I bid him adieu. I promised him continued prayer and told him that I would come to the hospital as soon as I got back in town. With that, I left and hit the highway.

Chapter 32

In just under ten long hours I was driving down my in-laws' street. Pulling into the driveway of their house and watching Teri come out to the yard was a welcomed moment. Walking over to me, she gave me a kiss and a hug through the rolled-down car window.

"You can't wait until I get out to properly salute me?" I teased. Getting out of the car made my stiff bones crack, yet they felt good as I stretched my arms toward the sky.

"I've missed you so much, sweetheart," she said as she grabbed and hugged me again and placed kisses on my neck.

"I've missed you also," I told her as I picked her up and spun her around once.

"I bet I missed you more."

"I don't think so, darling." I gave her a sad puppy dog face. "You just don't know how lonely that house can be without you there. This has been one long week for me."

"Come on in the house. Everyone has been waiting for you."

Her whole family was there waiting on my arrival. I said my hellos, hugged some, and shook hands with others, and then, not wanting to keep them waiting any longer to sit down for supper, I quickly went to the bathroom to wash up and change my shirt.

After her father offered praise of thanks for my safe journey and for seeing his whole family together, we ate the large bounty placed in front of us. We had glazed ham, baked chicken, cabbage, greens, macaroni and cheese, potato salad, and dinner rolls. For dessert, we had sweet potato pie and 7 Up pound cake. This was just what the doctor ordered after a long drive.

After we finished eating, my father-in-law, my brothers-in-law, and I continued to sit at the table and talk while the women cleared the dishes and cleaned up. We talked about the church and politics, the weather, our families, and anything else they could think of. I was extremely tired, and sleep was coming down on me with full force after my meal settled. So I graciously excused myself for bed. They all understood. I was still sexually charged from last night's encounter with Sharand. When Teri finally came to bed, I was able to show her just how much I had missed her.

"Randall, darling, you know my parents are just down the hall."

"Woman, I have missed you all week. Do you know how wonderful it feels to have you in my arms right now? We are just going to have to try to be as quiet as possible."

"You are a mess." She giggled.

"Yeah, baby, but I'm your mess."

We were acting like two high school sweethearts who were crazy in love.

"I love you so much, Mrs. Harris."

"And I love you too, Reverend Harris."

"Did you enjoy yourself this week, Mrs. Harris?"

"Yes, I did, but I missed you, Reverend Harris."

"All I did was lie around that lonely house and read all week, Mrs. Harris."

"It really sounds like you missed me, Reverend Harris."

"If only you knew, Mrs. Harris, if only you knew."

Drowsiness was overtaking both of us.

I had lied to Teri until my head hurt. I hadn't lain around the parsonage all week. And thinking about poor

Grace made the pounding more fierce. I glance over at
Teri, lying in my arms. Her eyes were closed, and she
was on her way to slumber. I wondered if she could see
through some of my lies. She was much smarter than I
gave her credit for. She knew me. I was just glad that she
was sleepy and didn't want to talk anymore tonight. I just
had way too much on my mind, including all the business
I had to take care of when we got back home.

Chapter 33

Saturday went by rather quickly. There weren't many visitors, which I was glad about. I wasn't up to becoming reacquainted with half of the South Side of Chicago. I'd see most of them in church tomorrow.

My father in-law, the Reverend C. I. Andrews, was the pastor of the Holy Road Baptist Church. He had already informed me that I would be his special guest minister for Sunday's services. I was ready for it.

Saturday afternoon I finally had time to fill Teri in on Grace Dixon. She was very concerned.

"Poor Brother Dixon! When we get home, I can do something for him. I'll make up a few dishes so that he can just put them in the refrigerator. That way all he will have to do is warm them up when he wants to eat something. That poor man has had so much happen to him within this last year. Hopefully, Grace will not be in the hospital very long. We are going to have to check in on them as soon as we get back home. I just wonder who would do such a thing like that to her. I don't know her that well, but she seems like such a quiet girl."

I let Teri talk until she got tired.

"I just hope the police can catch whoever it was before they get a chance to hurt someone else's child."

My stomach was getting that hollow feeling again.

"Yes, dear, I'm sure they will. Now tell me, what did you do all week?" I desperately needed to change the subject. Her comments were hitting me pretty hard. She went on to tell me about all the things that she'd done. About how happy she was to be home with her parents. But my mind was elsewhere. I didn't think I heard anything that she said.

Her parents were also glad that I was there. They doted on me like I was a child. They were such good people. During dinner that evening they tried their best to catch me up on the latest happenings in the Windy City and at the Holy Road Baptist Church. It was a pleasant visit, but I was anxious to get back home.

Sunday morning I woke up to gospel music coming from the radio, the smell of coffee brewing and bacon frying. For a quick minute I thought that I was a young boy back home at my mama's house. I hadn't had a chance to think about my mama very much with so much going on.

My mama had been a single parent and had worked two jobs to support my older brother, Anthony, and me. We grew up in Memphis, Tennessee, on the wrong side of the tracks, as they say. I had always loved church and had known that one day I was going to be a minister. But my brother had chosen a different road in life altogether. While I was going to Sunday school, prayer services, and revivals, Anthony was committing felonies and going back and forth to jail. Before he was finally sentenced to life in prison, he had already pretty much written me off as his brother. But he'd worried our poor mother to death, literally. After all her hard work and sacrifice for us, he just never seemed to appreciate it.

He would always find a way to blame her for our station in life. She told me that she wasn't able to go to school. That she had to drop out as a young girl to work after her own mother had died in Mississippi. However, she worked very hard to make sure that we had the opportunity to go to school. She would wake up before daybreak and leave the house. Sometimes we wouldn't see her until we were ready for bed.

When she wasn't cleaning house for that mean ole lady Mrs. Clarkson, she was cleaning house and tending to the spoiled, bratty children of Mr. Dewey Bolton and his wife. In the evenings, she would cook and clean up at a restaurant downtown. I remembered vividly how dog-tired she was when she got home, only to get up the next day to do it all again. No matter what she did, it was never enough for my brother. Anthony just never wanted to sit down long enough to listen to anyone.

Even still, a mother's love ran deep, and she worked her fingers to the bone to pay bail bondsmen to give him chance after chance. I made a promise during my sophomore year of high school that I was going to go to college, work hard, and take care of my dear mama so that she would never have to work like a dog, cleaning houses for someone else, ever again.

I saw myself as a minister of a big, beautiful church, and she would sit on the front pew with the rest of the mothers every Sunday in her white suits and big, pretty hats. But my precious mother developed type 1 diabetes, and she never told me. I found out later from one of her doctors. I had noticed that she was losing weight, and every now and then she would complain about problems with her heart. She was going to those county clinics, which everyone knew were not the best health-care providers. I promised her that if she would just hang in there, I would see to it that she got only the best doctors that money could buy.

My senior year of high school was going to be my best. I had girls asking me out on dates. I had football scouts watching me, and I had a college scholarship locked up. It was the first step in my plan to achieve success, and it was a very busy time for me. Well, it turned out to be my worst year.

My brother was involved in the robbery and murder of the owner of a men's clothing store. It just so happened that the victim was the patriarch of a very prominent Jewish family that did a lot of work in the fight for civil rights.

After he was convicted, Anthony was sentenced to life in prison without the possibility of parole because of his lengthy criminal record. Mama went and sat in court every day during his trial. I guessed her poor heart was just too weak and she simply couldn't take anymore. After his sentencing, her heart just gave out and she lay in the hospital for four weeks before she died. I didn't think that I was ever going to get over the death of my mother.

I hadn't written or heard from my brother in fifteen years. I had heard that he blamed himself for Mama's death. He had told a family member that he killed our mama just as surely as if he'd pulled out a gun and shot her himself. I agreed. As far as I was concerned, my mama was my only family, and now it was Teri.

I did think about my mama often, and even after all this time, it still hurt deeply. After all, she was supposed to be living with me and Teri in the parsonage, sitting on the front pew at Unity Missinary Baptist Church in her pretty hats, without a care in the world. But my selfish brother had taken care of that.

Teri's voice calling me to breakfast brought me back to reality. I wiped the tears that had formed in my eyes and went down to eat.

Like always, my mother-in-law had made a breakfast feast. There was bacon, sausage patties, hot links, scrambled eggs, eggs sunny-side up, hash browns, homemade biscuits, orange juice, and hot coffee. Too bad we didn't have much time to enjoy the delicious food before church services.

Her father would occasionally look up at me to ask me if I was enjoying myself.

"Yes, sir, I am most certainly enjoying myself." I would say and nod. We were able to talk about my church a little after the meal, while the women cleared the table. Then I had to excuse myself so that I could get ready for church.

The Holy Road Baptist Church was packed. The choir sounded a whole lot better than it did the last time its members squawked their way through the services. The congregation was made up of mostly older members who had been there for a while. My sermon wasn't as intense as it usually got; it didn't have to be for his congregation. I preached about patience, about Abraham and Sarah. Something that I was sure they could relate to. They were not ones for all the whooping and booming words on fire. All in all, the entire church was very responsive to it, and Teri was proud.

"I am always more than happy to come and share the Word of the Lord with you," I said as I shook hands with people in the slow-moving crowd, my smile frozen in place. "Bless you, Mother. Bless you, Sister, Brother. . . ." *Okay, enough of this,* I thought. I was ready to get back to my in-laws' house.

I didn't eat much for dinner. My mother in-law, an extremely lovely woman who loved to pamper us whenever we were in her home, didn't seem to take offense. Because of the long drive ahead of us, I didn't want to make too many unnecessary stops. I wanted to hit the highway before three o'clock in the afternoon, so I told Teri it was time that we got going.

"You know I really don't like driving once it gets dark," I told her. But I knew that I would have to drive a couple of hours after the sun went down.

We all said our good-byes, and her mother gave us her famous travel package consisting of fried chicken wings, dinner rolls, ice water, hot coffee, wet, soapy hand towels in a ziplock baggie, and a roll of paper towels.

This had been a nice getaway. I could see that Teri was much happier than she had been in a while. But now it was time to get back home and back to business.

Chapter 34

My house never looked as welcoming, as inviting, and as comfortable to me as it did after a short trip. We got home after three in the morning. The highways were just a little more congested than I cared for them to be. Teri and I slept most of the morning away, getting out of bed after eleven. The drive had taken a lot out of both of us.

After showering, we left for the hospital to check on Grace. We didn't bother with breakfast, because I told Teri that we would probably have to make Brother Dixon eat something if he was in the same shape as he'd been in before I left on Friday. When we reached the hospital, it was a much different picture.

When we got to the waiting area of the ICU, we were in for the shock of our lives. We spotted Brother Dixon sitting in one of the lounge chairs, laughing his heart out. Sister Betty Gary was sitting next to him, and she had him laughing and talking more than I had ever seen him laugh or talk before.

"Well, well, well, I see that the Lord is still in the blessing business," I said and greeted them.

Teri and I took them both by surprise.

Sister Gary jumped up to hug us. "How was your trip, Sister Harris? Pastor, I was on my way to the church when I felt that I should stop by and check on Brother Dixon here. I knew you were gone for the weekend, so I just took it upon myself to keep an eye on him. I also wanted to see how Grace was coming along. I didn't realize this much time had passed." She looked down at her watch. Her mouth was going a mile a minute. I had to hold my hand up to interrupt her and tell her that everything was fine.

"You just have a seat and continue whatever it is that you are doing. I haven't seen our dear brother Dixon laugh like this in a long time." I clasped my hands together. "So what's the good news today?"

"Pastor, Grace has been downstairs all morning. She has been up and talking since yesterday! They are running a few tests, but the doctors say that everything looks great." He chuckled. "I tell you, the doctors say they have never seen anything like it before. But you want to know what I told them?" Without waiting for a response, he continued. "I told them that I serve an awesome God."

"Praise the Lord!" Teri threw her hands up in the air. "There is nothing better than coming home to wonderful news."

"The Lord is good," I said.

"The doctors say that she will need some physical therapy and that she will have some trouble walking at first, but they have full confidence that she will walk again and everything without any problems. Isn't that wonderful? At first they had thought that her spine was more damaged than it was, but thank God it wasn't," he went on. "She should be able to come home soon."

Not wanting to ask in front of anyone but knowing we would probably never have the chance to be alone, I asked him if he had heard anything about the baby.

"She was pregnant?" Sister Gary interjected in surprise. Brother Dixon and I both ignored her.

"Well, before she was able to speak or anything, the doctors and I both agreed that it was best that they go ahead and take the baby. I hope that the Lord will forgive me, but I didn't know what else to do. She was about two months along," Brother Dixon informed us sadly.

Looking up at me for reassurance, he continued. "The doctor felt that it would be harder on her if she kept the child, considering what her poor body was going through. But they do feel it's a miracle the way her body has pulled through after they removed the fetus. The doctor did not remove her uterus, and she feels pretty good that she will not have any problems in the future. But he has advised her that she should not try to get pregnant any time soon." He wiped his forehead with the back of his hand. "I can agree with that." He tried to smile.

"I'm sure the doctors made the right decision," I assured him. "And as you stated earlier, we serve an awesome God. He is a forgiving God, and He forgives all of us."

"Have you eaten anything today?" Teri asked him.

"No, not yet," he answered. "I was sitting here, talking with Sister Gary, and we just lost track of time. I'm hungry, though."

"Oh, call me Betty, Brother Dixon." Sister Gary giggled like a schoolgirl.

"Only if you call me James," he told her. This made her giggle even harder.

"How about lunch on me?" I offered. "And you don't have to worry about the church this morning, Sister Gary. You come along with us. I'm sure whatever you have to do at the church can wait."

"I would be glad to join you all," she said as she eyed Brother Dixon.

"We can go to Annie Mae's if you feel like some good home cooking," I said. "Have you left the hospital yet?"

"Yes. I went home yesterday to shave and take a shower. But I don't think I want to go anywhere until they bring Grace back from her tests," Brother Dixon replied.

"Will you be more comfortable if we eat in the hospital cafeteria? It's your call," I told him.

"I just don't want to go too far away, just in case she may need something. You understand?" His eyes were pleading.

"Of course we understand," Teri assured him. "You don't have to explain." She took him by the arm. "Come on. We can go to the cafeteria."

On the way to the cafeteria, my heart felt lighter than it had in days. I was so happy that Grace had pulled through and that Cornell hadn't hurt her any more than he did or, worse, killed her. Or should I rephrase that and say, "Cornell and I"?

Chapter 35

After lunch we sat around the waiting room area and talked for a while. Sister Gary was all over Brother Dixon. Funny thing, he didn't seem to mind at all. Teri and I laughed about this the entire ride home. We were laughing so hard that we couldn't get out of the car. We sat in the sun, enjoying each other's company.

"Do you think I should still offer to cook a few things for him while Grace is still in the hospital?" Teri asked me.

"I'm sure that poor Brother Dixon has got his hands full with Sister Gary."

We both continued to laugh.

"You know something? She might be good for him," she said.

"You have got to be kidding me."

"No, think about it. He was laughing it up at the hospital when we walked in. He appeared to be having a great time. She may be the one to bring him out of his shell, and he may be the one to tone her down a bit."

With that statement, we both had to laugh again.

"What are your plans for the rest of the day, sweetheart?" I asked her. My mind was now on other things.

"I plan to clean up your house."

All I could think about was swinging by the pharmacy to grab a minute with Sharand. Maybe she had had time to think while I was away.

"What are you going to do today?" she asked me.

I gave her my sincerest look. She had caught me off guard, and I couldn't come up with a lie quick enough. "I don't have much to do today, and I will be home soon. I just need to make a run. I want to spend my evening with you." I kissed her on the lips.

"Then hurry back, darling," she said, getting out of the car.

I loved the fact that Teri never questioned my comings and goings. She didn't have to. She knew that I was always coming back home to her.

Driving out of the driveway, I questioned myself. Despite what had just happened to Grace, here I went again, chasing after Sharand. I could tell myself over and over that I needed something extra. But was it that I was more like my brother, Anthony, than I care to admit? Was it that I was just as selfish as he was?

I tried not to think about it, because all I wanted to do now was to see Sharand.

Walking through the door of the pharmacy, I saw Sharand helping a customer, that wonderful smile fixed on her face. She didn't see me at first, so I pretended to read labels as I watched her work. Her smile quickly disappeared when she noticed me standing there, staring at her. She tried to go about her duties when she finished up with her last customer, as if I wasn't there, so I walked over to her.

"Reverend Harris, can I help you with anything?" She wasn't smiling.

"Yes, you can."

She chose not to reply to my answer.

"Talk to me," I said.

"Talk to you about what?" She looked around to see if anyone could overhear our conversation.

"About you and me." I grinned at her.

Sighing heavily, she rolled her eyes toward the ceiling, becoming irritated. "Reverend Harris, I surely hope that you are not going to come around here and bother me while I am at work." She clasped her hands together, trying to control the volume of her voice. She looked around to see if any customers were listening.

"I will if you refuse to talk to me," I told her, looking as serious as I possibly could.

"You can't do this," she whispered, almost pleading.

"I don't want to do this, but I will if I have to."

She looked at me as if she had so much more to say, but she just shook her head in disbelief.

"I just got back this morning. I'll be in for the rest of the evening, but you can give me your number so that I can call you tomorrow."

"No, you cannot have my number," she blurted out. Then she looked at me again in disbelief.

"Then I will be here tomorrow, when you get off." I stared into her eyes for a few seconds, then turned to leave.

"Excuse me," she said in her professional tone of voice. I turned to walk back to the counter. "Please tell me why you're doing this to me."

"I told you how I feel about you. I want you, and I usually get what I want. I guess you can say that I don't take rejection very well." I smiled wickedly.

"But I'm not rejecting you." She was trying her best to whisper, but her emotions were getting the best of her. "For goodness sakes, you are a married man!"

"I know what I am."

She continued to stare at me in disbelief. When someone walked up behind me in line, she sighed heavily and quickly scribbled her number on a piece of paper. I thanked her and left.

When I got home, Teri was cooking, and the smell of smothered pork chops and Pine-Sol hit me in the nose as soon as I walked in from the garage.

"Dinner won't be ready for another hour, sweetie. Why don't you make yourself busy until then?" she hollered to me from the bathroom.

She had that horrible black rag tied on her head because she was cleaning again. She always wore that thing when she cleaned. She knew it got under my skin. She made me so mad wearing that thing, and she knew this. Why did this woman do this to me? I had to shake my head. I could guarantee that Sharand didn't wear a rag on her head like some old housemaid when she cleaned her house. What message was Teri trying to get through to me? Sometimes she could get to me.

Chapter 36

It was a splendid Tuesday morning in summer, with just a hint of humidity in the air. The sun was bright, the birds were singing, and the flowers gave off a mesmerizing aroma. Sometimes I wished I could work outside.

When I got to the office, Sister Gary wasn't in yet, but Tyerra was there, quiet as a mouse.

"Good morning, Sister Williams. How are things going for you this morning?"

"Fine," she answered without looking up from the computer.

"How are your classes going?"

"Fine."

I could see that she was nervous and didn't want to talk.

"Is there something wrong?" I walked into the office.

"No, sir." She wouldn't look in my direction.

"You know that if there is something bothering you, you can always come to me, don't you?"

"Yes," she answered, still looking at the computer.

"Well, I had better leave you alone. It seems to me that you have a lot of work to do."

"I'm just busy this morning, Pastor Harris." She gave me a brief smile, quickly glancing in my direction. Remembering the lunch that we had shared in my office a week ago, I figured that had to be the reason for her change in demeanor.

"Tyerra, is there a problem with me? Maybe you misunderstood something that was said at lunch last week."

I waited for her to answer. I could see that her mind was working nervously and she was becoming visibly shaken. I felt I had better put her mind at ease. Quickly.

"I'm terribly sorry if I made you feel uncomfortable last week. I didn't mean to make you feel that way. I just thought we were close enough to talk about certain things," I explained. "Your family has been some of my most devoted members here at Unity. I would not want to compromise that in any way. And, most importantly, I would not want to hurt you. Do you understand what I'm trying to say, dear?"

I looked in her eyes to see if she was still shaken.

"Yes, I do," she said, looking down to study her hands.

"Good then. I think you are a sweet young lady, and I have the utmost respect for you."

She finally looked at me and smiled.

"I better get to my office and let you get back to what you were doing." I smiled back at her. "I have plenty of work to do myself. You enjoy the rest of your morning," I told her before exiting the secretary's office.

"I will," I heard her say in a more cheerful tone.

My narcissistic way of thinking had had me going places that I knew where way out of the extreme realm that I usually allowed myself to entertain. I couldn't mess with her, anyway. That family was too close, and her father would tear my head off. Maybe I'd give it another year or two before I tried to hit that.

Turning my cell phone on in my office, I saw that I had some missed calls. I would turn it off when I didn't want to be bothered or when I wanted to spend uninterrupted time with my wife. I made myself comfortable at my desk and checked the phone messages. Monica had left the first one. *Forget that horny heifer.* She wasn't answering her phone when I was trying to reach her last week. Madonna had also left a message. Now, she was a challenge. I had had to take her out for a few dinners and had had to buy her high-maintenance tail a few gifts before I could get into her bed. She wasn't very creative. Her talent was her energy. I might have to give her a call later today.

Checking my agenda, I saw meetings, meetings, and more meetings. This was an indication of a very busy week for me. I wouldn't have much time to spend with Sharand. I figured that I was going to have to do a lot of sweet-talking to get into her sheets, anyway.

"I wonder what sort of gifts she likes," I said, rubbing the hair on my chin. She had extremely good taste, if the looks of her condo were any indication. Yeah, she had expensive taste.

Maybe I would arrange to have some yellow roses with baby's breath sent to her condo this evening. Yellow would imply friendship, hopefully a strong friendship. Yeah, I'd start with the yellow roses with baby's breath, and then I would give her a couple of days to try to figure out what I would do next. I wouldn't even call her today, to keep her on her toes. I looked at the piece of paper that she had jotted her number on. She might just be the one to cause me to quit the others if she just acted right. I lifted one brow as I teased my goatee. She was all of them rolled up into one. She was classy, sophisticated, educated, and beautiful, very beautiful.

As I was sitting at my desk, thinking about Sharand, my door flung open and Sister Gary hurried in, making all sorts of a racket, more than usual.

"Excuse me, Pastor Harris, but I saw that your door was partly opened. I take that to mean that you aren't too busy," she said, pulling a chair up to my desk and plopping down in it. As she held her chest and tried to catch her breath, I waited to see what could possibly be on her mind today.

"Do you need to talk to me about something, Sister?" I was annoyed that she had interrupted my thoughts, but she would never catch on. She always seemed to do this.

"Yes, Pastor, I do. I'm somewhat embarrassed to talk to you about this, but believe me, I don't have anybody else to talk to." She was still trying to catch her breath. "You know that I don't have very many friends, at least not what I would call close friends."

"How can I help you?" I asked her. I wondered if she was going to keel over on my desk, with the way she was carrying on.

"Well, you are my pastor and all." She laughed nervously.

"Yes," I answered, puzzled.

"Pastor, I need to know what it is that I do that offends people so. Now, I don't feel like I come on too strong, but I just don't know." She shook her head. "I know that people around here talk about me and all, but I still try my best to be a nice person. Women turn up their noses at me, and I just don't know what to do. At first I just kept telling myself that I didn't care, that it didn't bother me. But, Pastor, it does. It really does. To be honest with you, it hurts. Now, I don't want to change churches, because I love Unity with all my heart. I know that I can't run from one problem into another one. I just wish I knew what to do." She looked down at the floor.

After a few seconds of uncomfortable silence, she straightened up in her chair and looked at me for an answer.

After thinking hard about how I would answer her, I finally told her that I didn't think she came on too strong. "But I do think you have somewhat of a forceful personality." I held up a finger. "That's not always a bad thing. There are a lot of people with aggressive characteristics. I will say that you're an honest person, and you are a very sweet person. Very nice. And, Sister Gary, you work hard for this church. Unity would be at a great loss to lose you."

This made her perk up.

"Now, as far as people talking about you, they talked about Jesus himself. What makes you think that they aren't going to talk about you—and me—for that matter? Besides, as long as people are talking, then you must be doing something right."

We both laughed lightly.

"You may not become everyone's friend, and you shouldn't try. Just be yourself and don't let anyone else change who you are. You will be happier with yourself in the long run." I took a deep breath for what I was about to say next. "You want me to be honest with you, right?"

She nodded her head. She looked like she wanted to cry, not knowing what I was going to say to her. It was touching; I had never seen her in such a vulnerable state.

"Well, the only problem I see that you may have—and, shall I say, that maybe some of the other women of the church may have—is your choice of dress."

Shocked, she didn't say anything. She continued to look at my face for advice.

"There is nothing wrong with your style of dress. Maybe I should clear this up. I feel that with you being a young, attractive single woman, you may tend to wear your dresses a little too snug for most," I said, embellishing. I tried to smile, so as not to make the already uncomfortable conversation more uncomfortable.

"Oh!" She waited for me to go on.

"This may make a few of the women of the church uncomfortable, especially the ones with husbands in the church."

"Oh!" she repeated even louder when she finally caught on to what I was trying to say to her.

"Sister Gary, I don't think there's anything wrong with you at all. You are an incredible person, and most importantly, you're a Christian. Sometimes a person tends to look at the cover of a book without reading it first. Those are the type of people that we are not going to worry about. Life is too short for that. However, maybe you should take into consideration the tightness of your dresses. If anyone has a problem with you from there on, then it's just that—their problem, not yours. I know for a fact that people will respond to you on a different level if you loosen up the dresses."

We sat there for a few seconds in silence while we studied one another. I could see that she was thinking hard about what I had just told her.

"Pastor, do you think I wear my dresses too tight?"

"It really doesn't matter what I think," I lied to her.

Looking at me with sadness deep in her eyes, she said, "Yes, it does matter to me what you think."

Curious, I asked, "Why do you say that?"

"Because you are my pastor, but you're also my friend."

This made me feel differently about her and see her differently. I was truly concerned for her.

"Well, Betty Ann Gary, I am truly honored to be your friend," I said, standing and walking around to sit on the corner of my desk. "But what is more important to me than the way that you dress is that you are a Christian."

"Thank you." She finally gave me a brief smile. "I appreciate your honesty and your advice." She got up from her seat to hug me tightly around my neck. Then she turned and walked toward the door.

"You are truly welcome."

She exited my office, and I couldn't believe I had just seen a whole different side of Betty Gary. She was really a warm and pleasant person, and what she did for this church, I was sure I couldn't find another to do. I figured that this conversation had been brought on because of her new friendship with Brother Dixon. I just hoped that she didn't change for anyone. And I meant that.

Chapter 37

I woke up with another one of my headaches. I popped a couple of the sinus tablets that Sharand had suggested at the pharmacy. Today of all days, I had a meeting at the Boys and Girls Club. I just hoped that it wasn't going to be a long one, with my head throbbing like it was. I couldn't see myself dealing with all those horny young boys and overdeveloped girls, all vying for attention.

I had had a glass of cranberry juice earlier, because at the time I hadn't had much of an appetite. That had since changed, so I swung into the drive-through at Hardee's and ordered a sausage biscuit. It seemed to hit the spot.

When I pulled into the parking lot of the Boys and Girls Club, the place was in rare form. Sometimes I had to wonder why we even tried to help some of these ignorant kids. I often wondered about the future of my people. Some of these kids did not even know how to behave; they didn't even have a clue. When I finally made it to the conference room, everyone else was there and the meeting was already under way.

After an hour or so of quarterly financial reports, fund-raising ideas, and after-school projects, the meeting was over and I couldn't wait to get out of there. I hadn't contributed much to the meeting, anyway. When I walked through the main lobby, I couldn't believe my eyes when I saw Raychell standing at the desk, filling out some papers. She never even looked up at me.

"Wouldn't you feel more comfortable sitting at the table, miss?" I asked.

"No, thank you. I'm almost finished," she answered before looking up to see who she was talking with. "Oh, it's you." She looked around to see who else might be hanging around.

"Yes, it's me." I smiled as wide as I could. "And how have you been, Ray baby? You sure do look lovely today."

Her eyes widened, but she didn't answer.

"So you're not speaking to me today? What's up with you?"

"Nothing," she answered, looking back down at her papers.

"I have missed you."

This made her look at me from head to toe. "You are so full of it," she said, shaking her head, then looking back at her papers again.

"What do you mean? What's up with all this animosity? You know how I feel about you."

"It's been three weeks since I've heard from you, and you have the nerve to tell me that you've been missing me. Please." She laughed. "I don't think so."

"Come on, Ray. This is not the appropriate place for a confrontation."

"You walked over to me, didn't you?" She looked me straight in the face with eyes that could kill.

"Why are you so cold?" She had never acted like this before.

"You don't really want to know." She went back to her paperwork.

"I want to know what you are doing at the club this morning," I demanded.

After eyeing me up and down for the second time, she said, "I'm filling out paperwork to become a volunteer. That is, if it is any of your business."

"Well, I am on the board here, you know."

Looking surprised, she replied, "I should have known. You're everywhere."

This made me laugh out loud, which, apparently, made her angrier. "You should remember that," I told her.

"Look, I need to volunteer this semester in order to graduate in the spring. But if I have to deal with you, I should probably look for another organization." She sighed.

"You don't have to do that. I would never interfere with your education. I've been helping you out for all this time, haven't I?"

Biting down on her bottom lip and looking past me to see if there was anyone around who could be listening, she seemed to be thinking of what to say to me next. "It's not like you didn't get anything out of the deal," she whispered. "And I have been doing a lot of thinking."

I braced myself for what she had to say.

She sighed and shook her head before going on. "I have been thinking a lot about myself and what I want."

By this time a group of kids was passing by, walking slowly and staring. I was getting annoyed.

"This is my last year in college," she went on, "and I will be graduating in the spring. I just need to move on. I have wasted enough time and feelings on you, and it hasn't gotten me anywhere."

"I helped your butt through school, didn't I?" I could feel myself getting angry.

"You know what I mean."

"No, I don't know what you mean. Tell me what you mean," I demanded.

"Look, I have found someone else and—"

"And my black butt," I snarled, cutting her off.

"Lower your voice," she whispered, looking around. "You don't own me, and like I said, I have found someone else. He is good to me, and he doesn't deserve this. Now that's that." She balled up the papers. "I guess I can hang this place up."

"I don't care what you do, but you owe me something."

"I don't owe you a darn thing," she shot back.

"Do you think that you're just going to take my money all this time and walk away from me like that?" I asked her, more angry than hurt.

After walking closer to me and staring me in the face for several seconds, she replied, "You're darn straight I am. You never gave a damn about me." She pointed her finger toward my face. "You used me like a whore on the street, and I am sick of the whole game." Gritting her teeth, she continued. "You do not own me, all right? Now, get that through your thick head. Go home to your wife, Reverend Harris, because we both got something out of this deal. My cookies weren't free. You had to pay to play in the cookie jar." She smirked and quickly turned serious. "Now, stay away from me, because I am sick and tired of being the reverend's whore."

Throwing the balled-up papers in the wastebasket next to the desk, she finally took her eyes off of me and walked through the glass doors and out of the club.

I was so mad by this time that I could have snatched her right then and there. I didn't care that people had started to stare. *I'll deal with her later,* I told myself. Nobody walked out on me. It was not over until I said that it was over, especially with some trick who had been taking my money all these years.

Chapter 38

I went straight back to the church, but I couldn't get anything done. Sitting in my office, I was still steaming mad about Raychell showing her butt the way she did at the Boys and Girls Club earlier. Everyone had left for the day, and I was glad, because I didn't want to be bothered. I didn't even want to deal with Sharand that evening. I was pretty much fed up with women and their bad attitudes.

Not able to get any work done, I decided to go for a drive to clear my head. Maybe I should swing over to 123rd Street to find some of Cornell's boys and see if they could hook me up with a bag of weed. If not, I would have to settle for a bottle of Hennessy and a pack of breath mints. Shoot, that crazy excuse for a grandson was so mad at me the last time I saw him, but I didn't care. I wanted to get a bag of weed so that I could go over to the Good Old Boys Club, sit back, and chill tonight. I wanted to get Raychell out of my mind, my system. I grabbed my keys and headed for the door.

When I reached the neighborhood, I couldn't help but think that it looked worse every time I came through here. They should really do something about this part of the city. Economic development, my butt. Nothing was going to help these worthless Negroes. Anyway, if they built something decent over here, they would just tear it up again. Driving down the littered streets, I could understand why anyone trapped down here would feel hopeless. This was a hopeless situation.

I couldn't find anyone who looked like they were selling, so I decided to go on home. I came to a red light and pulled out my cell phone. As I flipped through the numbers in my phone, all hell broke loose.

"Get out of the car!" He hit the window with the butt of the gun. I didn't even have a second to think of my next move. I was frozen.

"Now, nigga!" he yelled. I stared straight into his angry, confused eyes.

I thought that maybe I should try to drive off as fast as I could, and then—*bam*—glass shattered all over the front seat, hitting me in the face and neck. I saw what seemed like a quick flash of lightning out of the corner of my eye. I felt a sharp piercing in my left temple . . . and then everything went dark.

This cannot be how it is going to end for me, can it? I thought. *Can it, Lord? Carjacked in this dirty, crime-infested neighborhood, where I had no business being in the first place? Oh no. Poor Teri. How will she handle this?* My thoughts were going in every direction. I could feel my heart pounding as the blood poured out.

I couldn't believe it. I was being transformed. I could actually see myself slumped over in my car. And the guy who shot me? I would never forget those eyes. Those angry, sad, hopeless eyes. That scared bum was running; he was running away. Where were the po-po who rode up and down the street all day? It took a while, but people started to come over to see what had happened. I could hear a siren in the distance. Warm blood was spilling over my neck. This was it for me.

A couple of thugs relieved me of my money clip and watch before the police made it there. At least they left my wallet so that I could be identified. One of them had taken the few dollars that were in it and had thrown it back on the front seat. Things were happening so fast. Lights were flashing; people in uniform were running back and forth. Everything was so confusing. I didn't know what was going on. *Oh, Lord, it can't be the end for me. I have so much more to do. It can't end like this. It just can't end like this.*

Chapter 39

Wait a minute. . . . What is going on? I'm not dead yet.
I couldn't open my eyes, say anything, move any part of
my body, but I was aware and could hear everything that
was taking place. I was in a very white, very busy hospital
room with machines hooked up to almost every part of
my body.

The doctors were working fervently to keep them
beeping. I was lying on my back, and my head was turned
so that the left side was up. They were working with what
looked to be a white sheet over it, working through a slit
or hole in the sheet. I couldn't tell which.

*What in the world is going on? If this is how it is sup-
posed to end for me, why are they still messing around
with my head?* I could hear one of the doctors discussing
a bullet. He was saying that it was lodged pretty deep and
he would not be able to remove it.

What? A bullet in my brain?

They continued to talk. They were saying something
about me dying on the table if they tried to remove it,
that I could remain comatose if they didn't. Where in the
world was Teri? I tried to cry out, but I couldn't.

Now they were saying something about talking to her
and her making a decision. *Please, Teri, don't let them
kill me,* I was screaming, yelling, but only to myself. No
one could hear me.

After a long time, the doctors left the room, disappear-
ing through two large white double doors. I was left with

a few nurses and the beeping machines. These machines were making me crazy. I was left to lie there to try to figure out what was going on.

I must have been having some sort of outer-body experience. I could see it all clear as day. The doctors were speaking with my distraught wife in another room.

Teri had a decision to make as they explained to her what was going on. They found her in the lobby with a number of people from my congregation. Poor Sister Gary seemed to be more upset than Teri was. A few of them were genuinely concerned about me, I was sure, but some of them had come out because they were just plain nosy. The doctors explained the seriousness of my condition and what could happen if they went in and attempted to remove the bullet. They also explained the pros and cons of the bullet remaining in my head.

"He is stabilized right now," one of the doctors told her. "But you will need to make a decision within the next twenty-four hours," he warned.

The doctors left her alone in the small conference room. Deacon Sam Wise led them in a thunderous and moving prayer. Sister Gary fell on the floor. The group then dispersed. Deacon Wise stayed behind to comfort Teri. She had insisted that she wasn't leaving the hospital and going anywhere tonight. Old Deacon Wise and I were like two peas in a pod; after all, he was my right-hand man in crime. He just better not try anything with my wife.

Chapter 40

Several hours had passed, and I had never experienced this degree of loneliness before. The only company I had was the occasional nurse or two who came in to check my IV, check the machines, or to glance over at me for a quick second to jot something down on their charts. I had been praying and talking with God like I had never had to do before. But I just didn't feel Him around me. I didn't even think that He heard me anymore.

It was the next morning, and Teri was still standing vigil out in the waiting area. They wouldn't even let her come in to see me. I knew that if she were to come in, I could get her to understand me. She would be able to hear me. A few of my members had come back to sit with her and keep her company, and for that, I was thankful. She needed their support. The reverends Cole, Leonard, and Clay had all come out to see if they could offer any assistance. They were praying and talking, praying and drinking coffee, praying and laughing. Those preachers were really praying for my recovery.

Dr. Miller, one of the doctors from last night, came in to get Teri, and he had a new doctor with him this time. He was introduced as a specialist who had extensive experience in the type of complicated surgery I might undergo.

"Mrs. Harris," Dr. Miller said once they were alone, "this is Dr. Walter Steinbalm."

They all took seats in the smaller conference room. Dr. Steinbalm explained that the surgery was a very risky one to try, if she chose to have the bullet removed, because of the bullet's positioning. He explained that I had a good chance of surviving, with few side effects, if the bullet stayed in.

"I have had many patients in this position, and I can assure you, madame, that they are living fulfilling lives with few complications. Uncommon side effects would be seizures, blackouts, and severe headaches. There should not be any reason for him to limit his daily activities much once he is up and getting around." He smiled. "I have had several patients do just fine in this same situation," Dr. Steinbalm went on to explain. "Most of them without the severe side effects, I might add."

Teri did not say anything. She could only sit nervously and rub her hands together.

"I have to tell you, Mrs. Harris, that I do not feel comfortable going in after the bullet. It is in a very sensitive area," Dr. Steinbalm said, showing her a couple of X-rays and pointing to certain areas on the chart as he spoke. By the looks on their faces, I could tell that I was in a very trying predicament.

"So, Doctors," Teri finally said, "you do not feel that you can safely remove the bullet, right?"

"Well, Mrs. Harris . . . I may be able to, but I want you to understand that it is in such a position that if I were to move it a fraction of an inch either way, it could cause some very serious problems. Going into this sort of surgery, we are never certain of an outcome. Now, we can attempt it with your say-so, but it is totally up to you." Dr. Steinbalm paused to clear his throat. "On the other hand, we can hope that he is strong enough to pull through this if the bullet is left in place. And we can wait to see what will happen. This next couple of days are very critical for him. He seems to be fighting with all that he has, but I have to be honest with you. I am getting only very limited brain activity at this time."

Teri put her hands over her face and began to sob. The doctors walked over to her to give her a reassuring pat on the shoulder. She sighed heavily to compose herself.

"Oh, I don't know what to do! What would my dear Randall want me to do? I just don't know. I just don't know," she kept repeating to herself. I wanted more than ever to put my arms around her and give her the biggest hug to let her know that everything would be just fine.

"So, Dr. Steinbalm," she said, tears still streaming down her face, "are you saying that in your opinion you would leave the bullet where it is and see what happens?" She pleaded with her beautiful hazel eyes.

Taking her by the hand, Dr. Steinbalm sat next to her. "I am saying that I feel that we should see what happens in the next forty-eight to seventy-two hours. Honestly, I feel that the surgery would be much too risky." He was trying to be as comforting to her as possible.

"I understand," Teri said, wiping the tears from her eyes. "I will have faith that you will do your best possible job to take care of my husband, Doctors." She tried to smile, but it would not come. "I will wait it out and allow God to work."

"I think that this is best, ma'am," Dr. Steinbalm agreed, once more extending his hand to Teri.

"He is in the best of care, Mrs. Harris," Dr. Miller interjected. "Dr. Steinbalm is the best in his field." He extended his hand and laid it on her shoulder. "You should try to get some rest. We promise to take good care of your husband."

"Thank you, Dr. Miller." She touched the hand on her shoulder. "I know that you will." She finally was able to smile at both of them.

With this, Dr. Miller wrote something down in his chart and both doctors walked out of the conference room and disappeared down the long hallway. When Teri joined the others in the waiting area, she was glad to see that Mother Wiley had left her hospital room and had joined them.

Mother Wiley had been in and out of the hospital quite a bit lately. The church had been praying for her for some time. She was one of my dearest members. Although she was not an educated woman, she was so full of wisdom. I just loved to watch as she interacted with the young people of the church. Everyone just loved her. She told the most amazing stories about her life. One of her favorite jokes was that she had buried four husbands and that she was looking for number five. Sadly, these past few months hadn't been so nice to my dear mother Wiley.

She had discovered that she had uterine cancer and had told me that she was going to beat it, like she had beaten everything else that she was faced with in her life. I was sure that she would, but she was having such terrible reactions from the chemotherapy treatments. But cancer or not, she was sitting there in the waiting area, with her ever-present pleasant smile fixed on her face. Teri was relaying to all what she and the doctors had discussed and the fact that they felt that she had made the right decision.

"We are all just going to have to stay prayerful and allow the Lord to do His Will," replied Mother Wiley. "Because I have no doubt that my pastor will come out of this just fine. And when he is finished, we will all be thankful." She smiled. "God is not through with him yet. The pastor has plenty to do."

The room was quiet as Mother Wiley spoke, everyone listening intently.

"This little ordeal will not stop the work of the Lord," she said with confidence. "Sister Harris, you have been a devoted first lady and a wonderful example of a first lady. You carry yourself as if you were born of royalty," she teased. "Just stay humble, and you, too, will be blessed more than you can imagine. The Lord has so many blessings in store for you and the pastor. But sometimes if we do not slow down, He has a way of doing that for us."

You could have heard a pin drop as everyone hung on to Mother Wiley's every word.

"I'm beginning to get tired." Mother Wiley laughed softly. "Have you been resting, Sister Harris?"

"Not much, Mother," answered Teri.

"Well, I'm not going to insist that you go home and get some rest, but I am going to ask you to please try. Because if I was in your shoes, I would be right here by my husband's side myself. But I can promise you, you do not have tzo worry. Pastor is going to pull through, and it is not going to do him a bit of good if you are not well. Do you understand?"

"Yes, ma'am, I do," Teri agreed.

"Then, honey, try to get yourself some rest. I am going to go on back to my room now. I'm going to come back down later and check on you."

"Thank you." Teri smiled at her and stood to walk her out of the waiting room.

Before Mother Wiley returned to her room, she told Teri, "My dear, I am not worried about a thing. I have total faith that God is in total control of this matter. And as long as He is in control, we must hasten to His will and let His will be done. Now, remember that it is not *our* will, but His will."

Teri kissed her on her cheek and beckoned one of the congregants to help her back to her room.

"Bless your heart, dear," Mother Wiley was growing tired in her wheel chair. Before long she was taken to her room with the assistance of a nurse's aide.

Chapter 41

The doctors worked fervently to repair as much of the damage made by the bullet as possible. At least they would now allow Teri to come into the room to see me for short periods of time since I was still in the intensive care unit. My condition was still very much guarded.

The police had stopped in again to check on my condition, wanting to know if there was any new information on the shooting. I just lay there, unable to speak, move, or even open my eyes. I felt very strange, because I was aware of all that was going on around me. The police seemed to be more interested in figuring out what I was doing in that area of town rather than finding out who shot me. Everyone was probably wondering the same thing, but no one had the nerve to ask out loud.

I didn't know if this experience would change my wife or not. She had never questioned my comings or goings, my late-night meetings. She had never checked my pockets or my cell phone bills. She had never seemed to get bent out of shape when a sister in a short skirt would try to flirt with me after services. She had always been a very strong, confident woman. But we hadn't faced anything of this magnitude before. She had never come close to losing her husband.

The police were asking her so many questions that she seemed to be becoming frustrated. They were asking her the same questions over and over, as if she might know something. I was glad when my old buddy Detective Mike

Riley came to the hospital and told them to all get lost. He was aware of all my side activities, so I was glad that he had taken over the case. He explained to Teri that they had very few leads in the case, but they were following up on what they had. He talked to the doctors as well, and they told him that I hadn't made any improvements and that they wouldn't give him any more information than that. He sat with Teri for about an hour before he told her that he had to get back to work.

The nurses were still running in and out of my room, pushing buttons, changing IV bottles, writing things down on the charts, and talking over me as if I were already dead. I still couldn't do or say a thing. This went on all night.

Mother Wiley was back in the morning, bright and early, to talk with Teri. Sister Bailey, who was supposed to sit up with Teri and offer her support, was sound asleep on the couch in the waiting area, snoring rather loudly. I was surprised that she hadn't awakened half the intensive care unit. The nurses on duty were trying their best to be pleasant and remain professional. But every so often Sister Bailey would hit a note that sounded like a semi revving its engine right in the middle of the waiting area, which was only a few feet from the ICU. Her huge chest moved up and down as her lungs took in air and pushed it out. Poor Teri was so embarrassed but was too nice to say anything. Finally, Mother Wiley rolled over in her wheelchair and gently tapped Sister Bailey on one of her massive arms.

"Sister Bailey. Sister Bailey, dear."

Suddenly the snoring ceased.

"Wha . . . what is it?" Sister Bailey asked, trying to come out of a deep, groggy state. "What is it?" she repeated. She was struggling to sit up on the couch, but her top-heavy frame seemed to be still sleeping.

"Nothing is the matter, dear. It's just that I thought you would be more comfortable if you went home and tried to get yourself some rest," Mother Wiley suggested. "I can sit here with Sister Harris for a while. You have been here with her all night. Why don't you go on home and check on your husband and children?"

"Are you sure, Mother Wiley?" she said, trying to steady her body. "Because you know I don't mind sitting here with Sister Harris."

"I know that you don't, dear, but I am here now. Maybe you should go on home and check in with your family. Make sure that you get yourself some rest." She made a great point in a way that only she could.

Sister Bailey tried to stand and stretch. "Only if you are sure. Because you know I don't mind staying at all," she repeated, all the while gathering her purse and jacket. "I didn't get a wink of sleep on this old lumpy couch, anyway."

"I know you didn't, dear," said Mother Wiley as she peered at Teri from the corner of her eye.

Sister Bailey hugged them both and rushed to the nearest exit. I bet she was afraid that someone would ask her to do something or change her mind.

"If I hadn't wakened that child, she would have awakened the whole hospital." Mother Wiley laughed. "I had to do that on behalf of all the poor sick people in this place."

She had Teri bending over in laughter. She hadn't laughed in three days, since the day I was shot, and it was really good to see her laughing again.

Dr. Miller came to talk with Teri and told her that my condition had not changed in any way. The bullet was lodged in my left temple. It had ripped through the temporal lobe and rested very near a blood vessel, just fractions of an inch away. But the good news was that there was no infection, and some of the swelling had gone down.

"I'll check in on him in a couple of hours. If there are any changes, I have already made sure that they will page me right away," he told her and left the waiting area.

They allowed Teri to stay a few minutes longer when she came into my room. She couldn't do much, since I had tubes coming out of just about every opening of my body. She did have a peculiar smile on her face as she stared down into my face. Then she bent down by my left ear.

"Randall, darling," she said, "I don't know if you can hear me, sweetheart. I don't even know if you know that I am here with you. I don't know if you know that you are here in this hospital intensive care unit. But if you can hear me, darling, I want you to know that I love you and that I haven't left you. I am right here, and I will be right here until you come back to me. I want you to fight hard, baby. Fight to come back to me, please. Whatever you do, please don't give up. Don't give up on us."

I can hear you, Teri, my love. . . . I can hear you, darling. And I love you too, sweetheart, I cried out. Only she could not hear me. *Don't worry, angel. I will never give up on us. Oh, Teri, when this is all over, I am going to treat you like the queen you are. I love you with everything in me.*

Many days had passed. In fact, so many that I'd lost count. Lying there in that cold, over-sanitized room, with its white walls and curtains, was very lonely. The smell of disinfectant and cleaners was strong and aroused my sense of smell. The only high points were the few moments that they would allow Teri in to see me. She would come in and hold my hand or gently rub my face. The look in her eyes was of total and adoring love. She was holding up as well as could be expected. She had left the hospital only to go home, shower, and change her clothes. Then she was right back here at the hospital.

The visits from the church members and friends were dwindling. But they had their own families and lives to attend to. None of my special friends, like Sharand, Monica, Shaletta, or Raychell, came out to inquire about me. I supposed it would be in poor taste if they were to just show up. If it were not for Raychell breaking it off with me, I would have never gone looking for a bag of weed. I would have never ended up in that part of town, anyway—that is, until I started dealing with Cornell Hollis. I usually went to the Good Old Boys Club for what I thought I was in need of.

This was not Raychell's fault. How could I blame her? If I had taken myself home to my wife, where I belonged, I wouldn't be lying here in the hospital with a bullet in my head. I had just got caught up in my own game. Like Cornell told me, I was going to get mine. And he was absolutely right. I got mine. Here I was, fighting to survive.

Ever since I became pastor of a church, women had thrown themselves at me. I was so weak. I didn't know what the big deal was with women and preachers, but those women just seemed to love us. I should have known better. A wise old man once told me when I was in college, "Every time you play a game, someone has to win and someone has to lose." I hadn't lost yet, and I was going to fight with everything in me so that I wouldn't.

Chapter 42

After lying around this place these past couple of weeks, with only the constant beeping and ringing of the medical equipment as my companion, believe me, I had had plenty of time to rethink a lot of things. I had counted and recounted every tile in the ceiling over and over and had even made a game of it. And I had continued to think about what was waiting for me outside those starched white walls. What did I have to look forward to concerning my life, my ministry, my relationship with my wife and my friends? All of these things required a change.

Sometimes I thought that if I didn't get up out of this bed soon, Teri would get tired of looking down on me. Maybe she would soon tire of sitting here day after day, not knowing whether or not I would ever be able to hold her in my arms again. Yes, I knew that she loved me, but that might soon turn to pity. She would begin to feel sorry for me. I couldn't handle that. Before it was over, she would start to despise me. She deserved a man who was strong, vital, and one who could function. I wished I had never taken her love for granted the way that I had.

It was times like this when I wished we had started the family that she wanted so badly. But all I could think about was my own selfish desires. But we were still young enough to start a family. She would make a wonderful mother. She had so much love to give. She would raise our children to be well behaved, smart, and courteous. They would grow up to be strong and to have high self-esteem. She would raise them to be driven and to work hard so they would lead successful lives. Most importantly, they would grow up in the church, and they would know God. That was the type of life that she deserved—not one where she had to take care of an invalid for the rest of my days. Changing my diapers, feeding me, bathing me. No, no, it just couldn't be like that. I had to pull through this.

I was so appreciative of the hospital for making sure that Teri had everything she needed. They were making her as comfortable as possible.

One evening they allowed Mother Wiley into my room to see me. I didn't know how she had talked them into bending the rules for her, but that was our dear mother Wiley. Teri was grateful that Mother Wiley would stop in to see me. She had such an abundance of respect for the older woman, who was so full of knowledge and love. A nurse had told her that she could stay only a very short time and that someone would come to get her.

For a time she just sat there looking at me with a smile on her face. She began to hum a song very softly, as if she didn't really want to disturb me. I remembered what my mother used to say when I would ask her why she hummed so much instead of singing and using her wonderful alto voice. She would tell me, "Randall, my son, sometimes I like to hum because that way the devil doesn't have any way of knowing what I'm singing about. It's all between me and God." She would look at me with a confident assurance. Those were some of her happiest times.

I couldn't make out the song that Mother Wiley was humming, but it was a beautiful melody. And as if I was sitting up in my bed, waiting for her to come to me, she came over to my bedside and began to speak to me. Mother Wiley was considered gifted. Some called her a prophetess; others called her a seer. Whatever it was, she possessed a special gift of God.

Her sweet demeanor suddenly turned serious when she said, "Pastor Harris, I have been sitting here and meditating on you. You know something? I have been praying long and hard for you these past few weeks. Yes, sir. Me and the master have had some pretty intense conversations about you. I feel that I need to tell you something, young man. Sometimes when we get too busy to listen to what the Lord is trying to tell us, then He has to sometimes knock us on our bottoms to get our attention. We should never let ourselves get too busy for the Lord. Not so busy that He has to knock us on our bottoms."

She chuckled. "You may not know this, but you are a very special man. You have been chosen. The Lord has a job for you to do. I feel compelled to tell you this, but in no way is the Lord through with you yet. You were chosen a long time ago, before this world knew anything about you. You were chosen to do the work of the master, and nothing will hinder that. Nothing can stop that which the Lord has demanded us to do.

"You were getting a little beside yourself. Your desires of the flesh and of the world were coming between you and God's work. He knew that you were weak. He knows you because He made you. And He knows that sometimes the best of men can become weak. He also knows that the devil is busy trying to tear down what we, His children, are building in His name. We who believe in Him must totally trust, believe, and surrender our lives to Him.

"Pastor, we ain't got no time for his mess. Satan is a liar and ain't never known what the truth looked like. Now, the Lord never promised us that this life would be easy. But He did promise to be with us every step of the way. Hallelujah!" She paused for a few minutes, and I was on edge to hear what else the Lord had put on her heart to say to me. Then she began again.

"My dear pastor Harris, it is time for you to give up those worldly things. Do away with those things that have caused you to sin against the Creator. He has blessed you. You have a special blessing set upon you because people are drawn to you. But you have been using it all for the wrong purposes. You have the ability to look through people's defenses and see exactly what it is that they may need at the time. But instead of helping them, praying for them, you were preying on them. You were preying on their weaknesses. You must not continue to seek out their weaknesses for your own satisfaction. My dear pastor, preying time is over. For it is now time to pray. And from now on, we must work wholly for the Lord."

After she had said this, she began to smile again. "Now, you continue to rest, Pastor, because you have plenty of work ahead of you. I love you. Lord in Heaven knows I do. I'm sure that you know that I do too." She paused. "But the Lord loves you more." She began to rub my arm. She continued to smile, but tears started to roll down her face.

"There is another thing that is weighing heavily on my heart, my precious son. I know that you have a brother, whom you have not spoken with in almost fifteen years. I know how close you were with your mother. And I know that she made plenty of sacrifices for both you and your brother. Now you feel that he just threw it all back in her face and never appreciated the things that she did. He caused her a lot of heartache and a lot of grief, but your brother did not kill your mother. Your dear mother toiled down here on this earth long and hard. She worked hard as a soldier for the Lord, but, son, your mother was tired. Her body was just worn out, and she needed some rest. She was ready to go home. There was nothing else that she could have done for your brother, nothing at all. He had made his way for himself.

"With you it was a different story. She didn't have to worry about you at all like she did about him. She knew that you were going to be special, that you would live a blessed life. She knew that you had given yourself over to the Lord, and truth be told, she had given your brother over to Him long before she died. It is time that you get in touch with your brother so that you can break down the wall that has gone up between the two of you. Your brother needs you right now, and you need him.

"Go on and reach out to him. Forgive him so that the Lord can forgive you. And please remember this. . . . No matter what you have done in the past, this is a new beginning. Forgive yourself. Forgiving ourselves is sometimes the hardest thing for us to do. But if God can forgive us, who are we to say that we cannot forgive ourselves? Bless your brother with your presence. Let him know that you are still here for him. You and your wife are the only family that he has right now, and he needs the both of you.

"Now, Pastor, you go on and rest, because there is something else that I want you to do for me. I feel that you are the only one I want to do this. I am tired now, and I have been tired for a long time. I'm going to hold on, though, until the Lord calls me home." She pushed the nurses' button for someone to come for her. "It seems that they have forgotten all about me." She giggled. "They said I couldn't stay long, and then they go and forget all about poor old me.

"But that only goes to prove how the Lord works. I'm glad I had this time to sit and talk to you, to tell you what was on my heart. I don't know if I will get down here to visit with you again. Just try to remember everything that I told you. Yes, sir, preying time is over. Now it is the time to pray." She paused a few seconds. "But right now, Pastor, it is time for you to get some rest. Go on and rest. Yes, Lord, I thank Him for you, Pastor Harris."

She patted my arm just before the nurse took her chair to wheel her out of the room.

"Oh, he can't hear you, lady," said the nurse. "He is heavily sedated and can't hear anything you say to him."

"He hears me," Mother Wiley said, correcting her. "He hears me, and he understands."

"Okay, if you say so," said the nurse. "Anyway, I'll take you back to your room."

"Yes," said Mother Wiley. "I'm a bit tired now."

They disappeared through the door.

Chapter 43

It had been three long days since Mother Wiley came to my room. I hadn't been blessed with her presence since. Every time someone came through the door, my heart would jump, as I was hoping that it was her, and every time I was disappointed. I needed to hear more of her insight, her wisdom.

My time had been filled with thinking about the things that she told me that day. I felt amazed that she knew that I could hear her words. What was even more shocking was how she knew so much about me. How did she know about my life before I came to Unity? How did she know about the people I had been involved with? Those people whom she said I preyed upon for my own satisfaction? I had fooled myself into thinking that I was helping them, when all I was doing was using them. Like poor innocent Raychell.

When I met her, she was a sophomore in college and was looking for a job. She had filled out an application for just about every department store in the mall when I spotted her sitting at the food court, sipping on a cappuccino. I thought that she was very attractive, and I could see that she was frustrated about something, so I decided to strike up a conversation with her. After she hesitantly told me about her day, I lied to her and told her that I could help her. All Ray wanted was a job, and I through te evil of my flesh convinced her to let me take care of her, to let me be her sugar daddy. It was my fault that she had allowed me to use her body in exchange for her education.

Please, Lord, have mercy on me, I begged in my mind.

And Monica, poor confused Monica . . . I met her when I was supposed to be helping troubled youth. Instead of having their best interests at heart, I was sleeping with their caseworker.

Mother Wiley was right about me. I did prey on their sensitivity and naïveté. And Grace . . . Oh, my goodness, what had I done to that poor child? Oh, God in heaven, please forgive me. She did not deserve any of the things that happened to her. She came to me while she was in mourning for her mother. Just thinking about what I did to that poor child was sickening, horribly sickening.

To make matters worse, I had actually wanted to soil that sweet, precious little Tyerra Williams. I felt a pang in my stomach. And to think that I was working on, putting pressure on Sharand Lewis.

What about all the others I'd used? When I'd become tired of them, I'd pushed them aside without an explanation of any kind. Oh, Lord, I had to make amends.

I had to thank Mother Wiley for her words. For they were the words of truth, and they were powerful.

I want to be forgiven, Lord, so that I can do your will. I want to help those in need and to show true compassion. No longer will I prey upon the weak like a wild animal of the jungle. I will pray for the weak and will let them know that by your stripes they too can be healed. And that through you, Lord, all things are possible. That they can do anything. That all power is in your hands. That you, Master, are the truth, the light, and the way.

I want to tell them that you are a mind regulator for the confused mind. Let them know that you are peace in times of storms. That you, Lord, are a heart fixer for the brokenhearted. And that there is no pain in heaven or on earth that you, Father, cannot heal. I want to tell the world that they never have to be afraid again, and that if we only have faith the size of a mustard seed and are believers and doers of your Holy Word, we can have everlasting life.

I repent here and now, oh, Lord. I come to you today, Father, asking you to please forgive me for the wrongs that I have done against your people. I come to you, Lord, as humble as I know how, bringing to you my sins and transgressions, asking you, dear God, to take them away. For I know no one else who has the power to do so. I want to be broken down, Lord. Then I want to be rebuilt. I want to be wiped clean, made whole.

From this day forward, I want to be your true and humble servant. I want to immerse myself in your word, oh, Lord. My heart burns for a reacquaintance with the Holy Spirit. Oh, Lord, I wouldn't serve any other God. I want to let the whole world know that you are the one and only true and living God, and that I am your obedient servant—a true messenger of your Holy Word. I thank you, Lord, for your forgiveness. I thank you, Heavenly Father, for your mercy. I thank you, oh, most high God, for your grace. Thank you, Father, for another chance. Another chance to serve you.

Chapter 44

Lying around this hospital would have begun to take its toll on me mentally, but the visit from Mother Wiley had given me a new way of looking at things, as well as a new lease on life, a life that I was looking forward to. I had been giving a lot of thought to what it was that she wanted me to do for her.

At the moment, I could not speak or move, but I was willing to lie there and be patient because I knew that soon enough I would. I was going to wait on the Lord.

Teri had been keeping up her vigil here at the hospital, although it was beginning to take its toll on her. She looked very tired when she came to look in on me. Regardless, I knew that she wouldn't want to be any other place.

I was lying there in bed, thinking about all the things that I wanted to do for Teri to show her just how much I loved and appreciated her for standing by me without a complaint. My mind was also mulling over all sorts of wonderful things that lay ahead for me, the church, and my life when I noticed that my right upper thigh was itching. I then realized that I had actually been scratching it for a few seconds. I could move my hand—not much, but I could move it! This was the first time that I had physically felt anything since I had been lying here. I could even wiggle my big toe a little. Thank you, Lord! I was actually moving for the first time.

Slowly, I tried to move every inch of my body from the bottom to the top. Some parts moved slightly, and others might not have moved at all. But I didn't care at that point. I might have been moving only a fraction of an inch, but it felt like a mile to me. I wanted to scream, "Halleluiah!" but nothing came out. That was all right, because I had the patience to wait upon the Lord. I spent the rest of my time praying and making the movements that I could.

After about another half hour or so, a nurse came in to check on me. Funny, she never even looked at me, since they thought I was in a vegetative state. She never even noticed that my eyes were partly opened.

"Good evening," I managed to whisper with a very hoarse voice.

The nurse was so startled that she almost jumped out of her skin. Holding her chest, she turned to look at me. "Oh, my goodness," was all that she could say. She quickly poured me a cup of water and had me suck it through a straw.

"Yes, it is His goodness," I was able to say after swallowing the last of some of the best-tasting water that I had ever had.

"Mr. Harris," she gasped, sounding amazed, "I will be right back. I have to get the doctor," and she hurried from the room.

Soon Dr. Miller ran into the room, with the nurse right on his tail. Walking over to me, I could see that he had a look of total confusion on his face.

"Reverend Harris?" he said in the form of a question.

"Yes," I answered.

He let out a heavy sigh. "Please forgive me, but I'm just a little beside myself." He started looking over his chart. "The readings here don't show any changes, so you can somewhat understand our surprise." He then looked over the readouts of the machines.

I tried to nod my head to let him know that I understood, but it was difficult for me. It was then that I realized that I had a thunderous headache.

He was looking into my eyes with a penlight. "I know that you may feel confused and disoriented. You need to get plenty of rest, but I would like to run a few tests as soon as possible."

I was tired of trying to talk, and the thumping in my head made me not want to move anymore.

"I will go and tell your wife the good news. In a little while, I will allow a short visit," he told me. "I must warn you that we have to be very careful at this critical point. I hope you understand. I wouldn't want you to have a relapse. And under no circumstances should you stress." He sounded stern. "Do not try to talk or overexert yourself, okay?" He placed his hand on my shoulder and smiled, looking me over once more. "This is an exciting day," he told the nurse as he checked my legs and feet.

"No, Dr. Miller, this is a blessed day," I said in a barely audible voice.

"Indeed, it is," he said and exited the room. "Indeed it is," I heard him saying as he walked down the hall.

It was about forty minutes later before Teri came to me. I couldn't tell if she was laughing or crying. Maybe it was a bit of both.

"Oh, Randall, darling! This is such good news," she said between tears. "I am just so happy, darling." She sobbed into my chest.

I wanted to reach up to touch her, to comfort her, but I was having difficulty. "I love you," I whispered in a raspy voice.

She held her head up and looked into my face as if she was in shock when she heard this.

"Randall, I couldn't believe it when the doctor came and told me that you were talking. I have been praying, and God has answered! For the past four weeks all I wanted was to hear your voice. I wanted to hear your voice so badly. I didn't realize just how wonderful it sounds." She began to cry again.

I could only try my best to smile at her to reassure her that everything was going to be just fine.

"The doctor explained that I shouldn't tire you out, but, honey, I don't want to leave you."

"Don't worry," I forced myself to say. I had to pause to clear my throat. I wanted to tell her that everything was going to be all right, but I couldn't. I was growing weak and couldn't speak anymore.

Smiling radiantly through her tears, she replied, "I won't." She stood and kissed me gently on my lips and across my face. "I don't want to strain your condition, so I had better leave. Get better, sweetheart, so that I can take you home and take care of you."

She looked at me with such intense love. All I could do was smile back at her. I wanted to reciprocate, but I was feeling so tired, and I took that as a sign that I was pushing myself. She just took my left hand into hers and massaged it. We didn't say anything for a long while; we just looked into each other's eyes.

Soon Dr. Miller came back into the room. "I really do hate to do this, Mrs. Harris, but we should let your husband get his rest now." He walked over to both of us and touched her on the shoulder. "We are going to set up some tests as soon as possible. We want to make sure that everything is working normally. I will tell you that this sort of thing doesn't happen often, and we are going to have to go about this very carefully. To be truthful with you, I feel that we still have a long hard road ahead of us. There will be long therapy sessions and a long recuperation process."

I was willing to work hard to get back on my feet. I was willing to do exactly what it took.

"I will allow you some time with him first thing in the morning," Dr. Miller told Teri when he saw that her face had grown sad. "I'm afraid that your visits will only be for short periods of time. You do understand?"

Teri agreed.

"I have contacted a few colleagues of mine, and a neurologist will come by in the morning. Dr. Makumbi is also a specialist in his field. He knows everything that a doctor needs to know about the brain. And he is also a superb neurosurgeon. I have more calls to make this evening. I'm sure that in a couple of days we will have everything set up. These tests will tell us everything we need to know for now. I'm sending a nurse to take some blood and urine samples. We won't bother you too much more tonight," he said as he checked my heart rate and pulse. Then he stood in the doorway, waiting for Teri to leave with him.

"I love you, darling," she told me as she leaned over to kiss my parched lips. Then she turned to leave with the doctor. I tried to gesture back at her, but I was so weak, so tired.

Chapter 45

This had been a busy week for me. If I wasn't being poked here, I was being jabbed with a needle somewhere else. I was hooked up to almost every piece of equipment in the facility. But you know something? All of that was all right.

After the long hours of tests, all I wanted to do was talk to everyone, to catch up on things. I was getting stronger and could hold a conversation without any problem, but the doctors would allow only immediate family in to see me.

Teri's family had wanted to come down to visit. But given his age, it was too far for her father to drive, and her mother had never learned how. And her sisters could not get any time off from work. She had assured them that she was all right and that all she needed for them to do was continue to pray for both of us. It was a hard job getting them not to come. But her father was not going to get on a plane, and she knew it.

My old friend Detective Riley had been out a couple of times to check in on me. He informed us that they were no closer to catching the person who had shot me than they were on day one. To be honest, I wanted to tell them to drop the whole thing, because in all actuality it was a blessing to me. This was going to put a stop to the harm that I'd been doing by taking advantage of those women. All because I felt that I was owed something that I'd missed out on as a young man. God knows that this was the only situation that could stop my narcissistic butt. Mama used to always say, "You want an earthly whipping any day than a whipping from the Lord." This was my whipping.

Mother Wiley hadn't been down to visit since that day, and I was becoming very worried about her. I had heard that her cancer had spread and that she wasn't responding at all to the chemotherapy. She hadn't been able to get out of her bed in weeks. Teri had gone up to her room to visit with her a few times and reported that her spirits were still high and that she was still thankful and full of grace. God bless her soul. Just as soon as the doctors said that I was able, I'd pay her a visit. Maybe I could talk the doctors into letting me go up sometime this week. I was sure Teri wouldn't mind pushing me up to her room in a wheelchair.

I was so disappointed when I was told by her doctors that I could not see her. They explained to me that her T cells were dangerously low and that she was at a high risk of getting an infection if they were not careful.

Since I was still not well myself, it was totally out of the question for me to see her at this time. All I could do for my dear friend was pray. Pray that we could continue the conversation that she was so sure I was listening to. I also wanted to find out what this important mission was that she wanted me to carry out for her. Because if the Lord said the same, nothing would stop me from doing whatever it was that she wanted me to do. I wanted to tell her just how much her words meant to me. How much she meant to me.

When I was able, the first person outside of my family whom I planned to speak with was Grace Dixon. I felt that I needed to speak with her as soon as possible. It was weighing heavily on my heart. I was told that she was home and was doing as well as could be expected given what she had gone through. After I told her everything and begged for her forgiveness, I was going to take a trip to the Pembroke Correctional Facility to have a long visit with my brother. Mother Wiley was right; I did need my brother right now. I wanted to get to know him all over again. My brother was the only earthly brother that I had. I had to let him know that I was wrong for blaming him for our mother's death. We had a lot of years to make up for. Yes, I had a lot to do when I got out of this hospital, but I had to concentrate on getting stronger so that I would be able to carry out the duties that lay ahead for me.

It felt so good to finally be able to relax in my own bed. It seemed like years since I had last seen my beautiful home. The past six weeks had gone by like a blur. The first week I was home, my congregation and friends were gracious, stopping by only to bring food, help Teri around the house, or run an errand or two for either of us. But my mind constantly stayed on Mother Wiley. I didn't get a chance to see her before I left the hospital, thanks to doctor's orders.

Deacon Wise and his wife stopped by this evening, after we returned from a therapy session. Sister Wise had prepared pot roast with potatoes and carrots, a pot of fresh green beans straight out of her garden, and a German chocolate cake. We had such a wonderful time laughing and talking while we enjoyed the delicious meal. Sister Ernestine never was a woman of limited talent when it came to the kitchen. That was obvious when you looked at her and her children. The deacon worked too hard to build up his business to pack on the pounds the way the rest of the family had, I guessed. He filled me in on all the business of the church and said my associate ministers and deacons were all doing a marvelous job running the church while I was away.

The congregation really came together during this trying time and showered me with undying love and support. They had supported Teri to the utmost. For this, I could not express my gratitude enough.

While she spent so much time with me at the hospital, some of the sisters would get together and come to the parsonage to water her plants for her. They kept the house dusted and tidy. And despite her defiance, they even cleaned out and restocked the refrigerator. They even took care of some of the laundry, vacuumed, kept the mail and newspapers in order, and did anything they could think of when they found out that I was coming home.

Later on that night, Teri and I were sitting up in bed. I was surfing the channels with the remote, and Teri was reading one of her books. I couldn't help but think of all the limitations that had been placed on me. I was walking with the help of a walker, but much slower. I got bad headaches, and I had to lie still until they subsided. Teri had to help me in and out of the tub, as well as wash me from head to toe. Teri had to help me do almost everything, because I was nearly helpless. There were very few things that I could do for myself, such as feed myself. I clicked the television off, hoping that she would put her book down so that we could talk.

"Honey, is there something I can get for you? Are you comfortable?" She placed her book in her lap.

"No, sweetheart, but I would like to talk to you for a moment, if you don't mind."

Concerned, she said, "Sure. What's the matter?" She placed a bookmark on her page, closed her book, and placed it on the night table.

"I know that I've told you that I love you so much, but I want you to know just how much I appreciate you also. You were at the hospital every day, and you never complained—"

"Darling, I am your wife," she interrupted.

"I know that," I said, searching for the right words to get my point across.

"What is it, Randall? Did the doctors say something to you at therapy today that I should know about?"

"No, sweetheart, it's nothing like that. It's just that I have . . . I have been wondering, is all."

She remained quiet, waiting for me to finish my statement.

"It's just that I have been doing a lot of thinking lately. I know that I haven't been the best husband to you, and I have sometimes taken your love for granted."

"Randall, please . . ."

"No, Teri. Please let me finish." I held up my index finger. "I need to say this."

She shook her head as I carefully selected my words before continuing.

"I sometimes wonder what in the world I did to deserve such a wonderful wife like you."

She released a deep sigh as a partial smile swept over her face.

I told her that she had always been the best wife to me. She had never questioned my comings and goings. She had never nagged or complained to me, and she'd kept an immaculate home. She made sure my meals were hot and ready no matter what time I walked through the door. Plus, she had my clothes clean and laid out for me. I admitted that I had been selfish when it came to her.

She nodded her head.

"When I first saw you in college, I knew that you were the one for me. I knew that first day that I wanted you to be my wife. You were the woman that I wanted to spend the rest of my life with. You were so beautiful to me then, and you are still every bit as beautiful to me now. I guess what I want to know is, why? Why did you put up with me and all my foolishness for so long? You have never said no to me. You have always supported any and everything that I've done one hundred percent. You followed me to a new city, where neither one of us knew a soul. Never once did you complain. You studied hard in college to work on your career in social work, and yet you have put your career on the back shelf for me." I was becoming emotional, and my words were getting caught in my throat. "I sometimes wonder what I did to deserve you."

After a long pause, she only smiled once again, never saying a word.

I went on, my voice cracking. "Teri . . . I promise you that I will never take you for granted again." My words began to choke me up again.

She began to speak with a tender calmness. One that I had seen before, but not often. It was one of the things that I loved so much about her.

"Randall, darling," she finally said, her smile still in place, "I know you love me, and that's enough. I never had to question your comings or your goings, because when it was all said and done, I knew who you were coming home to. I have never told you this, but my mother took me aside before we got married and had a long talk with me. She shared some important advice with me."

She chuckled. "My mother told me that the wife of a minister was one of the most difficult positions in the world. She told me that there were going to be a lot of ups and downs I was going to have to face. That my faith was going to be tested several times. But the most important thing for me to remember was that I was representing an elite brand of woman and that I was to always, no matter the circumstance, carry myself with dignity and grace. She then told me to be honest with her before she looked deep into my eyes and asked me if I thought I could handle the job.

"I was confused at first as I thought about what she had asked me. She explained to me in as pleasant a way as she could some of the things that I would face as the wife of a minister. Then she asked me if I truly loved you, and without hesitation I told her yes. Then I began to think about all the things that made me fall in love with you. It was all the little things at first. You used to walk around campus with your nose stuck in your books. Well, that was when you weren't playing football. I saw how driven you were. Nothing could stop you once you made your mind up to do something.

"You don't know this, but sometimes I would just sit back and watch you. How you would put your whole heart into your work, into what you believe in. You see, I know the true Reverend Randall Creighton Harris. You have allowed me to get to know that man. This is the man that I told her I was deeply in love with. And then I told her yes. Yes, I could handle the job. I just hoped that I would be able to handle it with all the dignity and grace that she has.

"Randall, I am not a stupid woman, and I believe you know this. I don't have to tell you some of the things I have witnessed right here at Unity. Women are and have always been in awe of some men in your position. But what keeps me standing by your side and supporting you, my love, is that I know who the real Reverend Harris is, and I will always know who it is that he loves. Now, please don't worry yourself anymore about this subject. I made a vow to you before God and our family and friends. I promised to you my everlasting and undying love and devotion."

I couldn't hold back any longer. The tears were burning my face as they streamed down. She gently wiped them away with her thumbs.

After I was able to compose myself, I said, "I want to make a trip to Pembroke as soon as the doctors allow me to travel. So we are going to have to get that paperwork in order."

"Pembroke?" she replied with both shock and excitement.

"I think it's time I talk to my brother, Anthony. I think that it is finally time for the both of us to sit down and get to know one another again."

"I think that is such a wonderful idea. I would love to finally meet your brother. You don't know how long I have prayed for this."

"*My brother,*" I said. "You know that it has been a long time since I have said that."

"Randall, I think it is a marvelous idea, and I would can't wait to finally meet your brother."

"So, you will go with me?" I asked her.

"Of course I will go with you. You don't know how long I have prayed for this."

"He has crossed my mind a few times over the years," I admitted to her. "I can't wait to see Anthony again."

She laid her head on my chest, and we sat like that until we fell asleep. When I awoke the next morning, we were in the same position. And even though I didn't think it could be possible, I was even more in love with my wife.

Chapter 46

It was an gorgeous autumn day, and the leaves were turning a vibrant red, orange, and yellow, which I loved so much to see. Sometimes, I'd get in my car and ride for long hours in the country just to look at the trees, because the city didn't offer this breathtaking type of scenery. Fall was my favorite season of the year. It was neither too warm nor too cold, and there was a certain crispness in the air that was invigorating to my lungs.

I was so happy when the doctors gave me the okay to travel. But only if I traveled short distances between stops and Teri did the driving. After all, I had been home only a month. The Pembroke Correctional Facility was a good nineteen-hour drive. We decided to make it a little getaway, a sort of mini vacation for us.

Teri drove the first leg of the trip, and when I felt myself getting tired, we stopped. We had made reservations before we left home at the Hyatt Regency Suites for the first night, and the suite was gorgeous. It was a bright, airy three-room suite with a plasma television and a Jacuzzi.

Poor Teri was worn out from driving, so the spa tub was just what she needed. After eating a late dinner in the hotel restaurant, we stayed awhile to enjoy the live entertainment. The vocalist performing was a beautiful young lady with a sultry voice and a style that reminded me a lot of the late Phyllis Hyman.

Everything was so nice and relaxing. When we got back to the room, Teri agreed to soak in the spa with me.

I was looking for something to put on and asked, "Teri, did you pack a pair of shorts or something I can use in the Jacuzzi?"

"No, dear, I didn't. Why do you need shorts? There is no one else here, is there?"

"I guess I don't really need them," I said as I stepped into the spa.

I hadn't been able to make love since the incident, so I was a little self-conscious. Teri, with her loving heart, had been understanding and patient with me. She was attentive to all my needs and doted on me like I was a helpless child. I was feeling nervous and couldn't figure out why. She wouldn't force me to perform or anything, but I couldn't help feeling nervous about being totally naked in front of my wife.

The warm water was calming, and she found a movie on the large plasma television as we both relaxed and allowed the jets to massage our bodies. Oh my . . . it felt so good. Like a thousand tiny fingers moving up and down my body.

Teri rested between my legs and laid her head against my chest. I could feel that she wasn't quite as relaxed as she should be, so I started massaging her shoulders.

"Your neck and shoulders are so stiff," I told her.

She didn't respond; she just let me continue to knead her neck and work on her shoulders. "Mmm, that feels so good," she finally said, moving her head from side to side. She was really getting into the massage. "This is so great, mmm," she continued.

Her moaning was beginning to arouse me. The more she moaned, the more I was getting turned on. She was so into her massage, I thought she didn't realize that for the first time since I left the hospital, my flag was at a full salute.

"Teri!" I said excitedly. "Look at what you've done!"

Sitting back and looking up at me, she had the biggest smile on her face.

"You knew what you were doing," I told her.

She leaned her head back on my shoulders and awaited her kiss. Slowly turning her body to face me, she whispered, "Remember, darling, not to strain yourself."

"Baby, I feel like I can love you all night long," I told her, my voice trembling.

"Are you sure?" She sounded concerned.

"Yes, I'm sure."

She started to get out of the Jacuzzi, and I pulled her back down to me. I began to smother her lips, face, and neck with kisses.

"What are you doing?" She giggled.

I couldn't answer, for my mouth was on a mission as it found its way down to her nipples. The heat from the tub was no equal to the heat between the two of us. It felt almost as if it were the first time.

My heart was on fire as my hands explored every inch of her body. As we made love, she let out a moan that had been trapped down deep within. Her body stiffened with each thrust until it quivered and relaxed against the wall of the tub.

"Come on. . . . Let's go to the bed," I said.

Rising to leave the Jacuzzi, I grabbed a couple of towels from the side and wrapped one around her body. She started to pat herself dry.

"You look so beautiful," I said as I watched.

Throwing the covers back on the bed, I took the towel from her and laid her down. She pulled the covers up over our bodies as she shivered from the cool air coming through the window.

"Why are you getting so shy all of a sudden?" I joked.

"I'm cold." She shivered.

"Let's see if I can heat you up."

Before long we were entangled with each other. Once again we were making passionate love, our bodies becoming one, rhythmically moving until a tidal wave rose in my groin and was released. I had to lie back and literally catch my breath.

"Are you all right?" Teri asked. I could tell she was getting nervous.

"Yes," I said between gasps. "I'm not a young man anymore, you know."

She sat up, looking at me with concern all over her face. "I'm going to get you a glass of water," she said as she started out of the bed.

"Teri, honey, I'm all right. I just need to catch my breath, is all. Honest, sweetheart, I'm fine."

She got back in bed, but she wouldn't take her eyes off of me.

"Let's get some sleep now," I said, my breathing back to normal. "We have a nice little ways to go tomorrow, and I want to be plenty rested when I see Anthony."

Thoughts of the meeting with my brother filled the better part of my mind. As I lay in bed and my wife drifted off to sleep, I kept running a scenario over in my mind of what the meeting would be like. Would Anthony want to see me? He did okay the visiting forms. What would we have to talk about? Did he just want to see me so that he could make me feel guilty for cutting him out of my life?"

A cold chill ran down my spine, and my stomach became uneasy. I closed my eyes and prayed that the Lord would intervene. That everything would work out all right. I wanted to see my brother. I still loved my brother. I talked with God until I slowly fell asleep. I was drained emotionally from just thinking of what was ahead for me.

Chapter 47

The next morning I was ravenous from the night before, so we ate a heavy breakfast at a nearby IHOP before hitting the highway. I felt so good that I convinced Teri to let me drive.

"I thought that I proved to you last night that I was back to my old self," I joked.

"And you also gave me a little scare," she scolded, looking at me from the corner of her gorgeous hazel doe eyes. "I'm always going to be concerned with that . . . with that bullet still where it is. I know that the doctor said that you were okay. But that bullet in your precious head bothers me greatly." She let the look of worry take over her pretty face as she rubbed her right temple.

"Besides a dull headache every now and then, I forget that it is even there. You shouldn't worry yourself any," I told her. "Besides, the doctor said that there are many people in my same condition who are leading perfectly normal lives. As long as I am careful, I can also."

"I just don't like talking about it. Let's just change the subject, if you don't mind." I could see that she was getting irritated, and it was cute.

"I'm so glad that the traffic isn't too bad this morning," I remarked. "We should reach Pembroke by noon. I wrote a letter to the warden explaining the situation, and Anthony should've been informed about the visit this weekend. I hope everything goes well today. I'm getting nervous and excited at the same time."

"It will, Randall dear." Teri rubbed her fingers gently across the back of my neck. "I just know it will." She smiled tenderly.

At 12:20 p.m. we pulled up in front of the correctional facility. It looked like something out of a bad B movie—a huge monstrosity of limestone buildings surrounded by rows and rows of razor-sharp wires.

"This place had to have been built over a century ago," I commented to Teri.

I thought the place was so depressing, until I realized that this was a place where dangerous and violent criminals were housed. I was praying that the interior was a little more inviting.

After identifying ourselves and going through the intensive check-in process at the visitors' counter, we were led to the visiting room. I must admit that walking through the heavy iron doors, which slammed behind us, and listening to the clicking of the locks on the way to our destination was enough to make my skin crawl. I couldn't even fathom having to spend the rest of my life in a place like this.

One of the guards pointed out a table to us, and we quickly took our seats. We had been sitting there for about forty minutes, filling the time with idle conversation and studying the other inmates and their visitors, when I began to think that maybe Anthony had not agreed to meet with me. It was then that I noticed a guard pointing us out to an inmate.

When the inmate reached our table, I could not believe my eyes. Standing in front of me was not the brother I had tried so hard not to think about over the past fifteen years.

The Anthony that I remembered was six feet two inches of solid muscle, muscle that he had spent many years working on while going back and forth to jail. No longer did he have long, thick hair, which he would chemically process so that it flowed down his back and over his shoulders. No longer did he possess those dark, hypnotic eyes, which he would use to get whatever he wanted from his ladies. No longer was he my tough big brother, who used to run the hood back in the day. The man standing before me couldn't weigh more than 120 pounds. His hair was thin and as white as snow. And it was cut close to his scalp. His eyes sat deep in their sockets, and his complexion was at least two shades darker than the beautiful caramel hue he once sported. I rose to greet my brother.

"Anthony?" I said.

He took my hand and shook it as hard as he could. "It is so good to see you, man. You're looking good, man. I mean good." He stepped back to scan me from head to toe. "Just look at my little brother," he said with a huge smile that exposed very few teeth.

"Anthony, this is my wife, Teri. She has always wanted to meet you," I told him.

"I'm so glad I have the opportunity to meet you, Mrs. Teri." He went over to her side of the table and gave her a big hug. "I have always known that my little brother wouldn't settle for anything less than a beautiful Nubian queen." He continued to smile as he stared at Teri.

"Thank you," Teri returned, forcing a smile.

We were both still in shock over Anthony's appearance. It was obvious the three of us felt awkward, so I tried to keep the conversation flowing.

"So how have you been, Anthony?" I asked him.

"Little brother, I didn't think I would ever see you again, you know?" he replied as he took a seat across from us.

I nodded my head. "I know there has been some bad blood between us, and I have come here to rectify that," I informed him.

"No need, little brother. This is a brand-new day, a fresh start. Let's just start from this moment on, right here." He hit the table to make his point.

I finally smiled back at the small, frail frame sitting across the table from me.

"So how long can you stay and visit?" he asked.

"We can stay as long as you like," I answered.

"We can have two four-hour visits a week, but I don't get many visitors at all." He looked down, shaking his head. He was quiet for a few seconds. "So come on, man. Let's play catch-up. Tell me what you've been doing with your life. How did you meet and marry this beautiful lady here?" He kept looking at Teri.

"Well, I'm the pastor of a church with a congregation of about eight hundred members right now. I met my wife in college. I don't know where to start. So much has happened," I told him.

"You're a pastor?" he asked, surprised. "That's wonderful. You were always special, little brother. I have always known that you would do great things. You were a good kid, sometimes a little stubborn, but you were a good little brother. Yeah, man, you were Mama's pride and joy."

This comment struck a nerve, but I sat silently and listened while he spoke.

"I know she loved the both of us, but you were her pride and joy," he repeated, rubbing a sore on his chin.

"She sacrificed a lot for us," I added.

"I know, and believe me, I have had plenty of time to think over my life's mistakes. I have made many. Little brother, I can understand your being upset with me because of the choices that I've made. I can even understand why you blamed me for Mama's death," he admitted sadly. "I know I broke her heart."

"Yes, I did blame you," I told him.

"You know, I tried to dull the pain of that guilt so many times, but it always seemed to come back. For a long time, I would always see her face, and she was always smiling the way that she used to. Remember?" He paused as he seemed to reflect on the past. "I used to wish that I could just wither up and die." He shook his head. Pausing for a few more seconds, he looked up into my eyes. "You've heard the old saying that you should be careful what you wish for?"

I nodded to show that I understood what he was saying.

"Well . . . that . . . that was before I found out that I had contracted HIV. I found out a few years back, when I developed a serious lung infection. To be honest, I wasn't too shocked when the doctor told me." His eyes grew even sadder.

The table was silent as Teri and I looked at each other, shocked by his news. I didn't know what to say to him.

"That's when I really began to think about my life," he went on. "Just how much of it I have thrown away. I have spent the majority of my life locked up in places like this." He spit the words out like they were a bad taste on his tongue. "Locked up like a dog. I don't have anyone to blame for it but myself. Mama did all she could for us. I could just never accept what she gave us, because I always wanted more. More than she could give us, no matter how hard she worked. And it didn't matter if I had more, because I wanted even more."

His demeanor was no longer jovial; in fact, he had turned very serious.

"I now have full-blown AIDS, and the little bit of life that I do have left, I am going to have to spend right here, still locked up like a dog. To die like an animal. I guess what I'm trying to say is that so many times I wanted to die because I felt that my life didn't mean anything to anybody. I was just another stupid, ignorant black man

who fell through the cracks of society. I have nothing
to show for my life, and I have had no one to love me
since Mama died. I never married, and I don't have any
children that I know about. All I had in this world, little
brother, was you. You just don't know how many times I
wanted to try to find your address so that I could get in
contact with you. I just didn't know how. But God surely
answers prayers," he said, wiping away the tears that had
formed in the corners of his eyes.

He went on. "The way I see it, anger is an emotion. As
long as I felt you were angry, I still had something to hold
on to. When I first came to prison, I was a hard man, a
beast, a monster. I didn't care about anything or anybody.
But over the years this place has its way of mellowing a
man out, bringing a man to his knees. The way I see it,
you have to still have love for me to be angry with me." He
tried to smile . . . only this time it wouldn't come.

I smiled and continued to listen as he poured out his
heart.

"My lifestyle has brought this disease down on me,
and it will soon take my life. But the little bit of it that I
have left, I have dedicated to a program that tries to turn
young people around. Let them know that this is not the
life they want to end up with. This is not the way to go.
Hopefully, I can stop one young person from making
the same mistakes I have made. It may not be much, but
before I leave this earth, I want to make a difference to
somebody. Then I will feel as though my life will not have
been in vain, that I meant something to somebody." After
taking a deep breath to recover and compose himself, he
sat up in his seat. "Enough about me, little brother. I want
to hear more about you."

We sat there and caught up, and the time just seemed
to fly by. I filled him in on the latest happenings in my life
and told him about the shooting that had left a bullet in

my head. I told him about the months in the hospital and about all the wonderful support I had received from the church and the community. We took quite a few pictures together, and before we realized it, visiting hours were over. I hugged my big brother, and we told each other that we loved one another. We promised to write often. I told him that I would visit him as often as my schedule allowed.

"Life in this place is livable now," he remarked. "Now that you have come to see me, and I know for sure that you love me, I have the fight to make it."

"God loves you too, Anthony. In spite of what we do, He loves us, anyway."

"You don't think that it's too late for me?" he asked sadly.

"No, it's never too late. Let's pray," I told him as Teri and I each took one of his hands in ours. I prayed a prayer of thanksgiving for my brother. I was surprised that the guards did not interrupt us for being too loud. The other inmates and visitors sat quietly, and most happily joined us in prayer. As I looked into my brother's face, I saw that his eyes had lost their dullness and had begun to shine somewhat. "I love you, Anthony." I hugged him as tightly as his frail bones could stand.

"And I love you too, little brother," he said as the tears began to flow down his face.

Chapter 48

After we left Pembroke, we stopped at a nearby diner right off the highway to get some dinner. It was small but busy, an indication that the food must be pretty good. Judging by the crowd, I figured that it was the town's meeting spot, one frequented by the staff and visitors of the prison. We settled in a booth and checked out the menu, which was written in chalk on a board on the wall. The day's special was roast beef, garlic mashed potatoes with gravy, corn, and a dinner roll. Dessert was a choice of apple or peach pie. A blue-haired little old lady hobbled over to take our order, and we opted for the day's special.

While we waited for the not-so-nice waitress to bring us each a glass of water, I told Teri that I had noticed that she didn't have much to say earlier. "I thought you were excited about meeting Anthony?"

"I just wanted to give you both a chance to become reacquainted with one another," she replied. "I do think it was a nice meeting, though."

"Mother Wiley said before she became bedridden that it was time for us to renew our relationship. She told me that he needed me and that I needed him. And now I see what she meant. I can't wait to get back home so that I can go and see how she's doing. Remind me, please, to have a huge bouquet sent to her room. So, my beautiful wife, tell me what's on your mind."

"Oh, not much," she answered. "It has been such a long day. I'm just so happy that things went so well."

"Yeah, they did . . . but Anthony is dying. We should do something for him before it's too late."

"The fact that you're back in his life is a marvelous start," she said. "Now he has the brother back that he thought he had lost. Imagine having to think that your brother is mad at you just to have a part of him to hold on to? That's so sad. It's heartbreaking." She shook her head.

"I know. I thought he probably never even gave me a second thought. He used to be so selfish. He never thought of anybody but himself. But I guess he did love our mother in his own way. We never had a father around to teach us how to be a man. I was lucky that I had strong, God-fearing mentors in the church. His were in the streets." I took a deep breath and held it for as long as I could before I blew it out with force. "But a deadly virus such as AIDS will force you to rethink your life's mistakes. I'll just make sure that I'm here for him for as long as he is here with us."

"We will both be here for him," Teri added as the waitress placed our meals in front of us. "This food smells delicious," Teri commented as she smiled at the waitress. She finally gave us a smile. I guessed she was tired and overworked herself.

We were so worn out from the visit and the meal that we chose to find a room in town and get an early start in the morning. We found a motor lodge right on the same highway. It was small but cozy. My mind was running a million miles a minute. All I could think about was Anthony.

"I'll send him a study Bible and some scriptures that have helped me through some trying times," I told Teri as we were readying for bed. "I think that we should try to visit him at least every other month, because this is a long drive. Maybe some of the sisters of the church can put together a care package for him a couple times a year. Maybe his physical body is wasting away in prison, but we will see to it that his soul can forever be free. The holidays are coming soon, and maybe we can start working on a special package for him. I will start as soon as I get home."

I was talking so much that I hadn't even noticed that poor Teri had snuggled up next to me and was fast asleep. I was just so stoked about my brother, I guessed. *I better try to get some sleep myself,* I thought, but I was too excited.

Morning came quickly and I wasn't hungry, so we grabbed some doughnuts and coffee from the same diner as the night before and hit the highway. The weather was perfect, and the traffic was fair. The sun was high in the sky, and the awesome autumn colors were mesmerizing. This trip seemed to rejuvenate me.

We stopped once to gas up and grab something to eat. The drive was so enjoyable. We laughed, talked, listened to music. With only a couple of stops for a fill-up and a bathroom break, before we knew it, we were driving into the city limits. When we reached the house and parked in the driveway, we remained in the car and prayed and thanked God for a wonderful, fulfilling, and safe journey.

Chapter 49

After a good night's rest, my next order of business was to go by and see Sister Grace Dixon. I ate a light breakfast of scrambled eggs and wheat toast and told Teri that I had some business to take care of and that I would be home soon.

When I drove up in front of the Dixon home all was quiet. The air held a cool sense of calm, which gave me the courage to do what I knew I needed to do. I stepped out of my car and took a good look up and down the street. Anything to give me more time to figure out what I was going to say to this poor woman. My heart was trying to beat through my chest, so I kept trying to fill my lungs with the cool fall air. I could feel beads of sweat form on my forehead in spite of the cool day.

My slamming the car door seemed to get the attention of someone in the house. I saw the curtains open and close. As I walked up the sidewalk, the front door opened. Grace stood there with a look of confusion and anger on her face.

"Good morning, Grace," I said to break the awkwardness.

"Ah . . . good morning, Pastor Harris," she said, now looking more confused than angry.

A few awkward seconds passed before I told her that I had come by to talk to her.

"That is, if you're up to it," I said, concerned.

"Sure. I guess." She moved out of the doorway so that I could pass.

She followed me into the living room. "Please excuse the mess," she said as she organized papers on the coffee table. "I was just going over some papers. I'm still thinking about going into the air force."

"Oh, that's wonderful!" I took a seat in a chair across from where she was standing.

"Dad thinks it's a good idea too. He says that he hates for me to leave, but he's willing to let me go if it's going to make me happy. I really hate to leave him, but he has started dating Sister Betty Gary from church," she announced as she sat on the couch.

This caught me off guard. First of all, Grace was in a pretty good mood, and then Brother Dixon and Sister Betty Gary were dating?

"When did this happen?" I asked.

"I don't know," she said with a wave of her hand. "She keeps him busy, and most importantly, she keeps him happier than he has been in a long time. At least I don't feel like I have to worry about him as much."

"That's so wonderful," I told her. I wanted to go to her, to show her that I was honestly concerned. But I did not want to overstep my boundaries. I felt so uneasy. "Grace, how have you been doing?"

"I'm doing okay. I just get so bored sitting around here all the time. I need to find something to do while I wait to hear from the air force. So far I've passed all the medical tests, which Dad didn't think I would be able to do. I have to admit I was nervous about that part myself." She sighed.

"Good luck in whatever you decide to do, Grace. I sincerely mean that." The room grew quiet, and the awkwardness returned. "Grace, I wanted to come by and talk to you about something. Before my incident, I know what happened to you."

"I figured that my father came to you, with you being our pastor and all."

My palms began to sweat. "What I have to tell you may cause you to hate me. All I ask is that one day I hope you can find it in your heart to forgive me." My eyes were pleading with her.

"What?" A look of horror flashed across her face. "What are you saying?"

"Grace, when you got pregnant and you started threatening me, I panicked. I got so nervous and scared. I began to see everything that I had worked so hard for go down the drain. I did something so stupid, so crazy," I admitted, my eyes still pleading with her for some sort of mercy. "This kid that I know told me he could knock you around and make you lose your baby." I could no longer look her in the face after making that confession. "Please believe me, Grace. . . . If I knew that he was going to hurt you like that, I wouldn't have ever let him go through with it. I'm so sorry."

She sat up straight on the couch, fear all over her face. "What if he comes back and tries to hurt me again?" she whispered.

"You do not have to worry about him. I have taken care of the whole matter. And he knows that he went too far. I don't think that he will be coming around either of us for a while." He didn't want me to see it but he was just as scared as I was. I looked into her sad, helpless eyes until I could see that I was getting through to her. She took a deep breath, and I allowed her to release it before I added, "Grace, I didn't mean for it to go as far as it did, and I will do anything to make all of this up to you."

She could only shake her head in disbelief.

"Name it, Grace. Do you want me to go to the police?" I asked.

Still shaking her head, she looked at me and asked, "How could you do this to me? I could have died. I . . . I just can't believe that you could have done that to me." She was understandably in tears.

"Grace, I was a different man then. When I got shot, I lay in that hospital bed and I realized the pain that I had inflicted on some people. And if it takes the rest of my life, I will go to each and every one of them and beg them for forgiveness. I almost died myself, and I now know just how precious life is. I had no right to do what I did. I first went to God, and I asked him for forgiveness. Now, Grace, I am coming to you to ask you for yours."

We sat there for about two whole minutes, just staring at each other, not saying a word.

"This is just too much," she finally said.

"I understand." I dropped my head in shame. "I don't blame you if you hate me. I know it'll take time before you can even begin to consider forgiving me, but please think about it. Hate only hurts the one carrying it and holding on to it." I felt like a hypocrite, saying these words to her.

She looked as if she was in deep thought as I spoke. After a while, she took a deep breath and released a heavy sigh. "Pastor Harris," she began, "I'm a different person also. When I got pregnant, I was scared myself. I feel that I need to be honest with you now." She stood up and walked over to the window. I was somewhat afraid because of the coolness of her demeanor. I didn't know what to expect.

After I sat on edge for a few long minutes, waiting to hear what she was about to say, she continued. "I didn't know for sure if the baby was yours. I just figured you were in a better position to take care of it. I wasn't thinking straight, either." She placed both hands against her head and shook it for several seconds, as if to dislodge horrible memories. Then she crossed her arms to hug herself before she went on. I myself was on edge as she spoke.

"Before Mama died, I was going with a guy that she and my daddy did not approve of. He's one of those guys who really don't like to work. He didn't have any ambition at all. All he felt life was about was smoking dope and having sex. He was a bum." She shrugged her shoulders. "I knew Deon—that is his name—wasn't going to take responsibility. He wouldn't know how." She smirked. "He never even finished high school. He thinks he's one of those thugs out there in the streets." She fiddled with her fingers. "But I did find myself attracted to him." She laughed dryly to herself.

I was taken aback by this revelation. I could only stare at her now as she spoke. I didn't even think that I was breathing. This knocked me for a loop.

"I didn't love him, but when Mama died, I just wanted to feel close to somebody." Turning to face me, she went on. "So, you see, I wasn't completely innocent in this whole ordeal. I didn't think things through, either. I could've hurt someone myself."

I swallowed the lump forming in my throat.

"After I lost my baby, I just wanted to start over. Forget all about the past. I figured that if I go into the air force, I could at least try to make a decent career for myself. And Daddy does seem to be getting along just fine these days," she remarked casually. "I think it is time for me to do something. So, Pastor Harris, I guess I need to ask you for forgiveness too."

I stood and walked over to where she was standing in front of the window.

"God forgives us both. Who am I not to forgive you when I need your forgiveness just as much as you need mine? We have both sinned and fallen short. I'm sure that whatever decision you make in your life, you will be successful," I told her, placing my hand on her shoulder and looking into her eyes so that she could see my sincerity. "I didn't know what to expect when I came over here this morning." I waited a second for my words to sink in. "I just knew that it was something that I had to do."

She looked down at her bare feet.

"We never have to mention this again, Grace. It's all in the past. As far as we're concerned"—I motioned between the two of us—"it's a dead issue."

We stared at each other in silence as traffic drove by on the streets outside.

"Then there is nothing more to say, I guess. Dad assumes it was Deon's anyway."

I didn't know what compelled me to hug her, but I felt that she need it. She refused to hug me back. But I knew that things would soon be back to normal between us.

As I walked out of her house, I knew that both of us had gone through a change. I was glad that she was not going to press charges against me, but I was willing to pay the price for my actions. God was so good. He had worked it out so that I didn't have to walk that path.

Chapter 50

On the way home from Grace's, I noticed that I was near the pharmacy where Sharand worked, so I decided to stop in and see if I could talk with her. Walking into the pharmacy, I saw that it was a slow morning. I scanned the store and didn't see Sharand anywhere. I was about to turn and leave when I spied her coming out of the back office. She was reading some papers and didn't notice me at first. When she finally looked up and saw me, she stopped dead in her tracks as if she had seen a ghost.

"I'm sorry that I startled you, Miss Lewis."

"Good morning, um, Reverend Harris. How have you been?" she asked nervously.

"Fine," I answered her. "I was just wondering if you had a moment so that I could speak with you."

She looked around to see if anyone was coming. "I don't think that would be a good idea," she said, irritated.

"I just want to apologize for the way I acted with you."

"Oh?" She seemed to let down her defenses.

"So, can I have a minute of your time? I'll take a second if a minute is too long." I threw my hands up in surrender.

"I have to start my shift soon, but I guess I can spare a few minutes," she said, still a bit hesitant.

"Can I get you a cup of coffee?" I asked, pointing to the coffee counter in the store.

"That won't be necessary."

"Please, I insist." She didn't answer but allowed me to lead as we walked over and took seats at the counter.

"Miss Lewis, I don't know if you know this, but I have been through quite an ordeal lately. But the Lord through His grace and mercy has seen to bring me through it." I poured us two cups of coffee.

"Yes, I read what happened. I meant to ask you how you were feeling. You surprised me, sort of caught me off guard."

"Sure. I understand," I assured her. "I have been feeling wonderful these days, better than I have in a long time. Just glad to be alive." I smiled and took a sip of the steaming hot coffee. "The reason I stopped in this morning is that I realize how I may have made a negative impression on some people. I was supposed to minister to God's people. To preach and teach, not prey and have my way. I'm trying to make light of this, but there's no joking about it. God had to slow me down for a reason, and, believe me, I started listening to Him. I made a promise to myself while I was in the hospital that I was going to make amends to all the people that I hurt and offended."

"You didn't hurt me, Reverend Harris."

"Oh, but I did, Miss Lewis. I hurt your spirit. I believe that you may have become a member of my congregation if I had not tried to force my intentions on you. I want you to understand that God had nothing to do with the way that I was carrying on. That is not how a true representative of God represents himself."

"I do understand." She smiled, relaxing even more.

"So I want you to know that I am truly sorry for my actions, and I ask you to give me a chance to show you how a real man of God acts, a true Christian. I would like to extend an open invitation for you to come again and worship with us at Unity Missionary Baptist Church. I pray you will like it enough to make it your church home. That is, if you haven't already found one."

"I haven't," she admitted.

"I don't think you'll find any people as friendly as the ones at Unity."

She beamed and admitted, "I do love the choir."

Before long we were both sitting there laughing and having a delightful conversation.

She looked down at her watch. "I better get to work. It was nice talking to you." She extended her hand with that warm smile that she so often had on her face. "I'm glad to see that you're doing better. I was concerned about you."

"Thank you for your concern, Miss Lewis. Take care of yourself, and I will see you Sunday."

She turned and walked toward her workstation.

I decided to stop by my office before going back to the house. I hadn't preached a sermon since being released from the hospital. Although the doctors hadn't yet given me the go-ahead, I was feeling up to it. I felt great.

It was a little past the noon hour when I reached my office, and Sister Gary was there, along with Tyerra. They were both sitting in the secretary's office, and both of them were looking upset about something.

"Good afternoon, ladies. Did I interrupt something?" I was trying to read the sad expressions on their faces.

"Good afternoon, Pastor," offered Sister Gary.

Tyerra remained quiet as she looked up at me with tears in her eyes.

"Is there something bothering you?" My concern grew.

"I guess you haven't heard the news yet, Pastor," said Sister Gary.

"What news?" My heart was pounding.

"Yesterday Mother Wiley passed away."

"Mother Wiley passed?" I heard myself repeat the words over in my mind. They echoed like they were trapped in a cave. I had to lean against the desk.

"Yes, sir," said Sister Gary. "You were still out of town, and we didn't have any way of getting in touch with you. Your cell phone was turned off. Someone called the parsonage this morning, but you had already left."

I took my cell phone out of my jacket and realized that I hadn't turned it back on since leaving the prison yesterday. "Does my wife know?" I sat in the chair across from Sister Gary's desk.

Sister Gary nodded. "Yes, sir."

"I see. Well, do you know what funeral home has received her body?"

"She's over at Patterson's Mortuary, the one on Eighty-Seventh and Freemont."

I could feel myself growing sad, and even more so, I was feeling sorry for myself that I wouldn't have her around anymore. Maybe it was selfishness.

"She didn't have any close family," Sister Gary went on. "You know that she considered the church to be her family."

"Well, Sister Gary," I said, trying to gather some inner strength, "we are going to have to make this the biggest home-going celebration this church has ever witnessed. This shouldn't be a time for mourning. We should be celebrating her illustrious life." I knew they were just words for that moment, but I was going to work on this and believe in what I was saying. I still had a lot of work to do.

Chapter 51

These past few days seemed to go by in one big blur. There was so much to do. I decided to let one of my associate ministers, Reverend Hill, preach the Sunday service since Mother Wiley's funeral was the next day. I had opted to say only a few words. So much had been on my mind lately that I had found myself constantly praying to the Lord for strength. But like Mother Wiley had once told me, the Lord was more interested in how we reacted when we were going through life's trials and tribulations. That was how He determined who was weak and who was strong.

I didn't get a wink of sleep the night before the funeral. I just kept going over and over in my mind the words that I would say to eulogize my cherished friend Mother Wiley. The morning of the funeral it felt like butterflies were fluttering around in my stomach as I stood in front of my bedroom mirror to give myself a once-over. I wanted to get over to the church early so that I could say farewell to my dearest friend in private. I saw through the bedroom window that the hearse had brought her body to the church over an hour earlier. When I saw them pull the casket from the back, my stomach dropped a few inches at the realization that the day was finally here.

A little later I told Teri that I was going on over to the church to check on things before the service got under way. Trying to settle the queasy feeling rising in my chest, I took deep, steady breaths of air as I walked slowly toward the church, as if I could put off the inevitable. As I walked, I looked up into the sky and saw that the sun didn't even want to make an appearance today. Only gray satin draped the sky, the air was still, and the birds were not singing as usual, for all were in mourning today.

When I reached the church and walked inside, I stood in the back. I could see that they had opened her lovely pearl-white casket, trimmed in silver for viewing. They had a large arrangement of calla lilies going across the entire front of the church. Calla lilies were her favorite, I was told, and they made a magnificent picture.

I stood there for a while, taking it all in, as a warm, peaceful feeling seemed to take hold of me. I had been telling everyone that this was going to be a big home-going celebration, but I hadn't actually felt it until now.

I walked up the aisle toward the open casket, and the closer I got, the more my heart wanted to rejoice. No longer did I feel sad that she was not going to be a part of my congregation anymore, a part of my life. No longer did the selfishness of wanting her to be here to share her wisdom take over. Yes, I was going to miss her greatly, but now she was at peace.

She had battled cancer for a long time, and not once had she complained. When I got to the open casket, I could not believe my eyes. My dear mother Wiley looked at least twenty years younger, as if she were lying there sleeping. She had the most pleasant expression on her face.

"Oh, Mother Wiley," I heard myself saying. "If only I had had the chance to tell you what your words meant to me. How they have helped me to see and understand the wrongs that I have done and the people that I have hurt. Mother, I have changed my evil ways, and I have realized the jewel that I have in my wife. I wanted to thank you for pushing me to mend my broken relationship with my brother. You were right. He does need me, and I surely need him. I know you knew I could hear every word you were saying that day. Those words will stay with me for the rest of my life. You will truly be missed, but I don't feel I have lost you. For I know exactly where you are. Resting in the loving arms of our Savior.

"Save a seat for me, dear mother, for I will see you in the morning. There are tears in my eyes, but these are not tears of sadness. Oh, I don't know if you can hear me. These are not tears of sadness. But these are tears of unspeakable joy."

I knew this might seem funny to most, but it looked like her smile grew wider as I looked upon her. I was beginning to hear people coming into the church, so I went to my office to wait for the service to begin. I sat there at my desk and played her words over in my mind. *Forgive yourself, because if the Lord can forgive you, who is any man that cannot?*

"Thank you, Lord," I said aloud to myself as tears burned the rims of my eyes.

I walked into my office before the service was to begin. I needed to get my thoughts together. I allowed the time to pass as I listened to some of my favorite gospel songs on my CD player.

When I heard that the service was about to begin, I walked out onto the pulpit and saw that Unity Missionary Baptist Church was packed from the front to the back. There were so many people that some couldn't find a place to sit and were standing in the back. No one in the whole church seemed to be mourning. The ushers were standing at attention with fans in one white gloved hand and a box of tissues in the other. The choir began to sing "Never Could Have Made It," led by Brother Teddy Broderick's beautiful tenor, and the sounds overflowed the church. I allowed the words to fill my soul.

When the obituary was read, we found out that our dear mother was a humble woman. She had never bragged about the things that she had done in her life.

We were surprised to find that she had been an active member and organizer of our local chapter of the NAACP during the late fifties and early sixties. We never knew that she and one of her husbands had marched in Selma, Alabama, with the Reverend Martin Luther, Jr., and that she had gone to jail several times herself during this period. That she had organized and marched for the integration of our city's school system. That even though she was never able to have any children, she—along with her husbands—had sent over one hundred children to college. All those grown children who could make it were in attendance today.

We learned that there was an incident that she had had as a child and that she had later found that she would not be able to have children of her own, so she had opened up her home to pregnant young girls who had nowhere else to go. She did all of this on a washerwoman's salary. We found out that day that she had worked hard all her life and had done many wonderful things in her life.

When it came time for me to eulogize her, I looked out over the faces that filled Unity that day and my heart was overjoyed.

"Today, church," I began, "we have come together to celebrate the home going of a great woman. A humble woman who always met you with a warm smile on her face, no matter the circumstance. A God-fearing woman who believed in letting her work speak for her, who believed in sharing in all that the Lord blessed her with, no matter how great or how small. And she did it without complaint. She would open her home up to you just as quickly as she would open up her heart. I'm pretty sure that if she had lived back in the Bible days, she would have been a story in the Bible. It would be a story unlike that of Ruth, Sarah, and Mary, the mother of Jesus. She worked long and hard for the Lord, and now I can most certainly say that she has received her reward. That is why today we have come together to celebrate.

"We aren't sad for her. We may be sad for ourselves. For our own selfish reasons. We can no longer take advantage of her loving nature or partake in her wisdom. A true Christian like Mother Wiley is rare, hard to find. She was like a rare jewel, the brilliant rare purple diamond of Africa. If we are blessed, we will meet someone like that once in a lifetime. I am glad that I had the chance to know her. I am thankful to God that I got the opportunity to know her, because she definitely touched my life. She touched my soul.

"While I was lying in the hospital after being shot in the head, Mother Wiley came to my bedside one day to talk to me. Even though the nurses were telling her, 'He can't hear you, lady. He doesn't even know you are here.' She knew that I could hear every word she was saying to me." I was beginning to get emotional at this point and had to pause for a few minutes to regain my composure.

"She read me like a book, and she told me what was on her heart. What she told me that day will stay with me for the rest of my life, right here in my heart." I pointed to my chest. Then I shared with them what she had told me while I was in the hospital. "Thank you, Mother Wiley, and I thank God in heaven for placing you in my life." I stretched my arms upward.

I was so caught up that I hadn't realized that almost everyone in the church had risen to their feet. The soloist Sister Eileen Hill sang "Home Going," and her beautiful voice had the entire church standing and applauding. There were plenty of tears that day. But they were not tears of sadness—only tears of joy. As I looked out over the congregation of Unity Missionary Baptist Church, I felt like a brand-new man. And not just a man . . . a man of God.

To the praise of the glory of his grace, wherein he hath made us accepted in the beloved. In whom we have redemption through his blood, the forgiveness of sins, according to the riches of his grace.

–Ephesians 1:6, 7

Book Club Questions

1. Do you know any men of stature (including those who are not ministers) who are like Pastor Randall Harris?
2. Why do you think Pastor Harris was such a narcissist?
3. The women Pastor Harris pursued were so different from one another. Why do you think that appealed to Pastor Harris? How did he attract these women?
4. Do you think that Teri knew about some of her husband's activities? Do you feel that she was naive?
5. Do you believe Teri was sending her husband a message by wearing a black scarf when she cleaned her home? If so, what was her message?
6. What is your opinion of the church secretary? Do you know anyone like Sister Betty Gary?
7. Who do you consider to be women of strength in this story? Why?
8. How do you feel about Cornell "Cee" Hollis? Do you know anyone like him?
9. What was so special about Mother Wiley? Do you believe that she had the gift of prophesy? How did she know that Pastor Harris could hear her when she went to his hospital room to visit him?
10. How do you feel about Grace's confession? Would you have forgiven Pastor Harris so easily if you were her?

11. Do you think that Pastor Harris will revert to his old ways?

12. What are your true feelings about redemption? Is it possible? Do you feel that Pastor Harris came about true redemption? How?

UC HIS GLORY BOOK CLUB!

www.uchisglorybookclub.net

UC His Glory Book Club is the spirit-inspired brain-child of Joylynn Ross, an author and the acquisitions editor at Urban Christian, and Kendra Norman-Bellamy, an author for Urban Christian. It is an online book club that hosts authors of Urban Christian. We welcome as members all men and women who have a passion for reading Christian-based fiction.

UC His Glory Book Club pledges its commitment to provide support, positive feedback, encouragement, and a forum whereby members can openly discuss and review the literary works of Urban Christian authors.

There is no membership fee associated with UC His Glory Book Club; however, we do ask that you support the authors by purchasing their works, encouraging them, providing book reviews, and, of course, offering your prayers. We also ask that you respect our beliefs and follow the guidelines of the book club. We hope to receive your valuable input, opinions, and reviews that build up, rather than tear down, our authors.

What We Believe:

—We believe that Jesus is the Christ, Son of the Living God.

—We believe that the Bible is the true, living Word of God.

—We believe that all Urban Christian authors should use their God-given writing abilities to honor God and share the message of the written word that God has given to each of them uniquely.

—We believe in supporting Urban Christian authors in their literary endeavors by reading their titles, purchasing them, and sharing them with our online community.

—We believe that everything we do in our literary arena should be done in a manner that will lead to God being glorified and honored.

We look forward to online fellowship with you.

Please visit us often at:
www.uchisglorybookclub.net.

Many Blessings to You!

Shelia E. Lipsey,
President, UC His Glory Book Club

ORDER FORM
URBAN BOOKS, LLC
97 N18th Street
Wyandanch, NY 11798

Name (please print):_____

Address: _____

City/State: _____

Zip: _____

QTY	TITLES	PRICE
	3:57 A.M Timing Is Everything	$14.95
	A Man's Worth	$14.95
	A Woman's Worth	$14.95
	Abundant Rain	$14.95
	After The Feeling	$14.95
	Amaryllis	$14.95
	Anointed	$14.95
	Battle of Jericho	$14.95
	Be Careful What You Pray For	$14.95
	Beautiful Ugly	$14.95
	Been There Prayed That:	$14.95
	Betrayed	$14.95

Shipping and handling-add $3.50 for 1st book, then $1.75 for each additional book.
Please send a check payable to:
Urban Books, LLC
Please allow 4-6 weeks for delivery

ORDER FORM
URBAN BOOKS, LLC
97 N18th Street
Wyandanch, NY 11798

Name(please print):_____

Address: _____

City/State: _____

Zip: _____

QTY	TITLES	PRICE
	By the Grace of God	$14.95
	Confessions Of A Preachers Wife	$14.95
	Dance Into Destiny	$14.95
	Deliver Me From My Enemies	$14.95
	Desperate Decisions	$14.95
	Divorcing the Devil	$14.95
	Faith	$14.95
	First Comes Love	$14.95
	Flaws and All	$14.95
	Forgiven	$14.95
	Former Rain	$14.95
	Forsaken	$14.95

Shipping and handling-add $3.50 for 1ˢᵗ book, then $1.75 for each additional book.

Please send a check payable to:

Urban Books, LLC

Please allow 4-6 weeks for delivery